The Robbers

THE ROBBERS
Nina Bawden

LONDON
VICTOR GOLLANCZ LTD
1979

Text © Nina Bawden 1979
Illustrations and jacket © Charles Keeping 1979
ISBN 0 575 02695 2

Printed in Great Britain by Ebenezer Baylis and Son Ltd
The Trinity Press, Worcester, and London

For Helen Murdoch

Chapter 1

All his life, Philip had lived in a castle. Stout walls surrounded him, rising sheer from the grassy headland that looked over the sea, and the door to the tower where his grandmother had an apartment was secured by an iron bar that was locked into place every night. "Safe from robbers and pirates and witches and warlocks," Philip's grandmother used to say when he was very little and afraid of the dark. And when the idea of pirates landing their ship on the beach and climbing the walls on rope ladders scared him too, she taught him a special prayer to say, to keep him safe, and after that he slept sound.

His grandmother had always looked after him. She lived in the castle, in what was called a Grace and Favour Apartment, given to her by the Royal Family, because Philip's grandfather had been a famous General. A Soldier for the Queen, Philip's grandmother said, and put his photograph on the chest in Philip's room in the tower, next to the photograph of Philip's mother who had died when Philip was born.

Sometimes Philip was sorry he had never met his mother who had a friendly face. But when he looked at his grandfather, a stern man in uniform holding a plumed hat under his arm, he was quite glad he was dead. Philip had the feeling that his grandfather had been the kind of man who would tell you to stop what you were doing if he thought you were enjoying it. Philip thought that his grandmother, who was good at enjoying herself, was probably better off without him.

Philip and his grandmother were happy together. They liked the same things: cinnamon toast and mint ice-cream and hamburgers, walking along the shore looking for shells and bottles that might have messages in them from castaways on desert islands, playing backgammon and singing hymns in the evening, and watching the same programmes on television.

They both found the news rather tedious but they watched it because sometimes Philip's father came on at the end with one of his Special Reports about something important that was happening in another country. These reports were boring to Philip and although his grandmother told him they were very interesting and that he must pay attention, he thought she was bored by them, too. She listened while Philip's father was talking, but all she usually said at the end was, "He's looking well, his cold must be better." Or, "I'm glad to see he's having better weather than we are in England. Nothing but rain, rain, rain here, but warm enough there for him to go out without a jacket." Or, "Poor Henry, he looks tired tonight. It's a tiring job, Philip, flying about from one dreadful old war to the other, never a week in one place. I really don't know how he does it. He was such a delicate child."

Philip's father was his grandmother's son so it was natural she should be concerned about his health. But the real reason they watched his programmes was that at the end of them he always said, "Good night," then smiled, and said, "Good night," again. Philip's grandmother said, "That second *good night* is for you, Philip dear, to show he is thinking about you." When Philip was small he had believed this, and boasted about it at school, but by the time he grew older, by the time he was eight, anyway, he had decided that saying "Good night" twice was simply a habit his father had picked up, like his grandmother's habit of saying, "Yes, yes, *yes?*" when she answered the telephone.

Certainly, when his father came to visit him, which he did about three times a year, it seemed to Philip that he wasn't interested enough in him to remember to say "Good night" on the television. He didn't even seem to remember how old Philip was. He always said, "Hallo, hallo, Phil old love. Lord, you've shot up, haven't you?" as if it surprised him that his son should have grown while he was away. Perhaps that was why the presents he brought, the books

A*   9

and the toys, were too young for Philip. His father had
meant them for a much younger boy.

Philip was sorry about the presents. It seemed such a
waste. But he didn't mind that he saw his father so seldom.
When his grandmother's friends said, "Poor little boy, he
must miss his Daddy," Philip thought they were silly. You
couldn't miss someone you barely knew, after all. But he
always answered, politely, that his father was too busy to
look after him and that he liked living with his grandmother.
And sometimes, if his grandmother's friends still looked
at him sadly, he added, "Besides, not many boys are lucky
enough to live in a castle."

He thought that he would live there, if not for ever,
because his grandmother was likely to die before he would,
for as far ahead as he could comfortably see. Even when
his grandmother was really old, about a hundred, and he
would have to look after her, they would still be happy
together in their safe, round tower by the sea.

Just after Philip's ninth birthday, his father got married,
in New York. Philip's grandmother had a letter from
America with a photograph of him and his bride, whose
name was Margaret.

"We'll have to send them a telegram," she said. "I wish
Henry had told us before. We could have gone to the
wedding."

"It costs a lot to go to America," Philip said. "And you
would have had to buy a new hat and a new dress. That
would have been another expense."

"My grey suit would have done. My church suit."

"It's got a hole in the back of the skirt. I saw it last Sunday,"

Philip said. His grandmother's clothes often had holes in them that she hadn't noticed because her eyes were not as good as they used to be. Even when she did notice holes, she rarely mended them, which was why Philip hadn't bothered to tell her about the skirt before.

"Oh well, it's water under the bridge now," his grandmother said. "I wonder where they will live. He can't take a wife to that poky little place he's got in London. No room to swing a cat, by all accounts."

"Who'd want to swing a cat?"

Philip had hoped to make her laugh. Instead, she sighed. "It's just a saying. You get old, it's easier to use old words. Saves energy. I wonder what she's like, this woman, Margaret?" She sighed again, and frowned.

Philip said, "Patience is a virtue as you're always telling me. You'll have to wait and see, won't you? I expect they'll come to see you when they come back to England."

They came the next week, in fact; came and went in the middle of the day while Philip was at school.

"They were sorry to have missed you," his grandmother said, "but your father was due at the studios at four o'clock. He'll be on television this evening. Late, but you can watch it, if you like. He brought you a model vintage car."

Philip had given up collecting vintage cars six months ago. He picked up the packet and put it down again. He said, "What's she like? This woman, Margaret?"

"He calls her Maggie. She's all right."

Philip's grandmother looked and sounded vague. She wasn't thinking about her son's new wife. She got up from her chair, grunting under her breath as she often did when her mind was occupied, and went into the kitchen. Philip followed and sat on the table while she moved about, laying a tray, putting a kettle on and hamburgers under the grill. She bent to light the oven and said, bent back to Philip, "You're to go and stay with them next week."

"*No!*" Philip was outraged. Next week was the Easter holiday and it was planned out already. The end of term. Hot Cross Buns on Good Friday morning. The first picnic of the year on Saturday. Painted eggs on Easter Sunday, and the service in Canterbury cathedral. "I *can't!*" he exploded.

His grandmother straightened up. "No such word."

"There is! I've said it! Anyway, stay with them where? You said there wasn't room to swing a cat."

"They've bought a house in London. Your father's taken a few months off work to settle in."

"I don't want to go."

"Your father wants you."

"What's that got to do with it?"

"He's your father. You're his son." She sounded angry, Philip thought. She was so seldom angry that Philip felt uneasy.

He said, "I've never been away. Only to Canterbury. London's so *far!*"

"Couple of hours on the train," his grandmother said. "You'll be all right. Boys your age fly all over the world and think nothing of it. I'll take you to the station this end and they'll meet you at the other."

"Aren't you coming?"

She shook her head. A few loose hairpins flew.

"Why?"

His grandmother didn't answer. A smell of burning rose, and an orange flame leapt out from under the grill. She seized the pan.

"Ugh!" Philip looked at the charred hamburgers. "*Yukky.*"

"I'll scrape the top off. They'll be fine underneath."

"No, they won't. The burn taste goes right through. Can I have toast instead? With ketchup on it?"

"Did you eat your lunch at school today?"

Philip pulled a disgusted face. "Camel dung! Only they call it shepherd's pie. And tapioca pudding. They tried to make me eat it but I said it was against my religion."

"Neither true nor funny," his grandmother said. She tipped the ruined hamburgers into the bin; then sliced bread and put it in the toaster.

Philip said, "I won't go. I'll lock myself in my room. I'll tie myself to my bed. You can't make me. You're not strong enough."

"You'll go," his grandmother said. "You'll go and you'll be good. You'll do what you're told and you'll go to bed when they say, and you'll eat what they give you."

"Not if it's *fish*," Philip said. Sick rose in his throat.

His grandmother said, "If they give you fish, you'll eat fish."

She said nothing more until the toast was made, and her tea, and Philip's milk poured as he liked it, with the cream taken off. She carried the tray into the living room and put it on the table in front of the window. They looked out at

13

the sea which was high today, drowning the breakwaters and throwing shingle over the sea wall.

"A spring tide," Philip's grandmother said.

Philip spread ketchup on his toast and bit into it. The ketchup, sweet, with a sharp under-taste, oozed up through his teeth. He said, "I can't eat fish. And you know it."

His grandmother pushed her lips forward thoughtfully. Wrinkles puckered her mouth so that it looked like a worn, gathered-up purse. "I've let you be fussy, Philip. I don't care what I eat, so it's been no trouble to pamper you. As long as you understand that when you're away from home things have to be different. Look at it this way. Suppose you were an explorer, travelling in a wild part of the world. You'd have to eat what there was, and it might not just be a matter of having to eat because you were hungry. In some savage tribes, for example, sheep's eyes are considered a delicacy. If you were offered an eye by the chief of the tribe and refused it, he would think it an insult. He might slit your throat."

"My father isn't a savage tribe," Philip said. "Or were you thinking of Maggie? Is she keen on sheep's eyes?"

"Not as far as I know. It was just a general principle that I was trying to explain to you. And a useful suggestion. Think of sheep's eyes, and you'll find fish, or whatever else it is you don't like, a bit less of a struggle."

"I could just go without," Philip said. "That's no trouble to anyone."

"It's a matter of manners," his grandmother said.

She drank her tea. Philip watched her throat move as she swallowed. She belched gently as she always did after the first mouthful and patted her collar bone with thin, knobbly fingers.

Philip said, "You arranged this behind my back. Without asking me. You're a treacherous monster."

She put her cup down. "That's enough, Philip. You mustn't name-call your elders, even if they deserve it. Nor repeat things you've heard me say, like *this woman, Margaret.* Your father won't like it."

"I don't see why. She *is* a woman, isn't she? Not a man. Or a dog, or a cat."

"It doesn't sound right, from a boy. You speak too freely for a child, Philip. That's all right between you and me, but some grown-ups might think you were being impertinent. You've got to learn not to say what comes into your head. You've got to think first."

"I always think. I mean, you have to think what you say, or you couldn't say anything."

"That's true," his grandmother said. "But not the point, really. There are some things it's all right for you to think, but wrong to say."

She sipped her tea. Her eyes, which were very pale blue, like faded old jeans, were distant and broody. Philip wondered what she had meant. He said, "I'm never *rude.*"

"Not to my mind," his grandmother said. "But it's not my mind that matters. I'm old, I don't count, I don't want your father, or this woman, Margaret, to think I've brought you up badly."

She sounded anxious and Philip was sorry. He said, "Oh, all right, then. I'll go if I have to, as long as it's not for more than a week, and I won't let you down. I'll eat what they give me, even if I have to go and sick it up afterwards. I won't say what I think. At least, I'll think *six times* before I say it. What else have I got to do? You just think, and tell me."

She thought of a good many things over the next few days. He mustn't read at meals. He must sit up straight at the table and make polite conversation. He must go to bed when he was told, even if he wasn't tired, and if his father and Maggie had friends to visit them in the evening he must not expect to stay up for supper. If he woke early, he must wait in his room until Maggie called him for breakfast and he must never go into his father's bedroom without knocking first. He must try not to argue unless it was really important. He must keep his room tidy and change his socks and his underclothes every day and remember his teeth, and his prayers.

None of these things was difficult and it seemed to Philip that he would probably have thought of most of them for himself, anyway, but he didn't say so to his grandmother because it seemed to comfort her to repeat them over and over. He did say, once, "All these rules, you'd think I was going to *prison* instead of just for a holiday!" But although she smiled then, she looked worried almost immediately as if she was afraid there might be another rule she had forgotten to mention.

The worried look changed her; made her face thinner and older. The Last Day, the day he was going to London, Philip thought she looked really quite hideous with her mouth pinched up and the lines round it drooping downwards. It made him feel cross with her. She was fussing all morning, packing and re-packing his suitcase, counting socks and shirts, and sending him into the bathroom to scrub the back of his neck and his finger nails even though he had already washed thoroughly. When, just before they left for the station, she insisted on straightening his tie for the third time, and dabbing at his hair with a brush, he jerked his head back and said, "Oh, do *stop* it, can't you? You're making me angry looking so dismal and ugly! If you're not careful, the wind will change and you'll be stuck like it."

She didn't alter her expression except to pinch her mouth even tighter. She put the brush down on the hall table and picked up Philip's suitcase.

He said, "I can carry it, stupid. It's too heavy for you. I put some extra things in when you'd finished packing, some books, and one of my Jubilee mugs." He tried to take the case from her but she shook her head without looking at him and hung on to the handle.

They walked to the station in silence. Philip felt miserable. He had been unkind to her. But she was being unkind to him, wasn't she? Sending him off like this. Like a parcel! She hadn't even said she was sorry that he was going. Or that she'd miss him . . .

Perhaps she wasn't sorry, he thought. After all, the way she'd gone on this last week about good behaviour must mean that she couldn't trust him to behave properly. She must think he was rude and horrible. Perhaps she was glad to be rid of such a rude and horrible boy!

A lump came up in his throat as he watched her thin,

humpy back walking ahead of him into the station. He blinked hard and whispered to himself, low and fierce, "*I won't cry.*"

His grandmother bought his ticket and gave it to him when they had passed through the barrier. She said, "Put it in your breast pocket. Don't lose it. You've got your money safe, haven't you? And coins for the telephone in case your father isn't there when you get to London. And his telephone number on that piece of paper I gave you."

"I'm not a baby," he said.

"No." She looked at him down her nose. "Be happy, Philip."

His face had gone stiff. The lump rose in his throat again, almost choking him. He said, "I can't *make* myself, can I? I can make myself do all the other things that you told me, but I can't make myself *happy*."

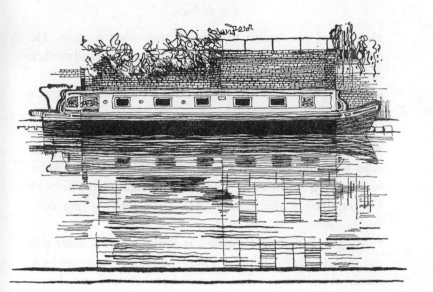

Chapter 2

His father ruffled his hair which annoyed Philip who had combed it just before he got off the train so that he would look smart arriving in London.

"Well, well, well," his father said. "Here he is, Maggie. What do you think of him?"

"He looks just fine to me," Maggie said. "Hallo, Philly. Glad to know you."

She was tall, as tall as his father with a round, flattish face like a pinky-brown plate and a thick, shiny, dark braid of hair hanging over one shoulder. She wore a long skirt and lots of beads and bracelets. Philip wondered if she were a Red Indian. There must be some Red Indians left in America.

He opened his mouth to ask her, then shut it again. He decided that this was the sort of question his grandmother meant him to think about before asking.

Instead, he said, "How do you do? You look very much younger than I expected."

He thought this was a polite thing to say. Besides, it was true. She did look young to have married his father who was quite old—over forty, and going bald. When he was looking stern, as he was now, he reminded Philip of his grandfather, the General. The same long, strong face, and big nose.

Maggie smiled. She glanced at Philip's father, who was not smiling, then winked at Philip. She said, "And you look much older. From what your father has told me, I was expecting a younger boy."

"He hasn't seen me for a long time," Philip said. "And I've always been small for my age. My grandmother says I will shoot up when I reach puberty. She says that's the way in our family. She says that my father was a skinnymalink until he was twelve and then he grew like a bean."

"That's a good word," Maggie said. "Skinnymalink."

"It means thin," Philip said. "It's not a word you'll find in the dictionary. My grandmother invented it, I think."

He thought of his grandmother and wondered what she was doing now. It was about tea time. She would be sitting in front of the fire, skirt hitched to the warmth, eating cinnamon toast and watching the children's programmes on television. Thinking about her made him feel weak inside. He could feel the tears coming and he looked down to hide them. There was a scrumpled up cigarette packet by his right foot and a torn piece of newspaper. He said, "My grandmother says people who drop litter about ought to be shot." And then, longing to hear her voice, "I ought to telephone. She'll be worried."

"I'll ring when we get home," his father said. "Come on, Phil old love, we'll get a taxi."

Philip sat on the tip-up seat and they sat opposite him. His father took Maggie's hand and held it on his knee. Watching them holding hands made Philip feel shy. He looked out of the window as the taxi went out of the station yard and round a big square with stone lions and fountains. "Trafalgar Square," his father said. "That's the statue of Nelson."

Philip looked up at Nelson, perched high on his column; then at the rest of the square. Trucks and taxis, cars and buses; huge buildings everywhere; hundreds of people and hundreds of pigeons. London. Londinium it had been called in the old days. Philip remembered his grandmother had told him to make polite conversation. He said, "The Romans and the Ancient Britons would be surprised to see London now, wouldn't they?"

His father and Maggie laughed and that puzzled him. He hadn't meant to be funny. He said, "I'm surprised, too. I knew it was a big city, but I didn't realise it would be so crowded and so full of traffic. It must be hard, crossing roads. I would be worried, looking after my grandmother. She's quite spry for her age, even with her sciatica, but she has tunnel vision. I keep telling her she ought to get a white stick for when she goes out without me, so that the drivers would know to be careful, but she's very obstinate. She doesn't want people to think she can't manage, she says. It's silly pride, really, and she ought to know better. After all, pride is a Sin."

He saw his father and Maggie glance at each other. His father pulled the corners of his mouth down and raised one bushy eyebrow. It was as if he were saying, *What did I tell you?*

Maggie said, "What is tunnel vision, Philip?"

"It's when you can see all right, quite sharp and clear, but only a bit, straight ahead. As if you were looking through a telescope or a tunnel. Grandmother says it's like being an old horse with blinkers. It doesn't worry her too much. Not as much as her back, though that's better, thank goodness, since we sent off for her Posture Cushion."

"Posture Cushion?" Maggie said. Her eyes were half laughing, half curious.

"It's a special kind of back rest that has a curved shape to hold the spine straight when you're sitting. I read about it in an advertisement and made her send off for it. That was last autumn and it was such a success that we bought one for Lady Anstruther for Christmas. Lady Anstruther lives in the apartment below us and she has a bad back, too, but it's been better since we gave her the Cushion. The pain is still there, of course, nothing can cure it, only Death can do that, Lady Anstruther says, but it has made the waiting more bearable."

Maggie said, "Oh!" The dark blood rose in her cheeks, making her look even more like a Red Indian. "Oh, you poor little boy!"

Philip wondered why she was sorry for him. He said,

"I'm all right. *My* back doesn't hurt. You don't get sciatica till you get old. The knobs of your spine start grinding together and pinching the nerves." He smiled at her kindly. "Don't worry about it. It's only what my grandmother calls fair wear and tear. I shouldn't think it would happen to you for a very long time."

"*You* shouldn't be worrying either," Maggie burst out. She sounded indignant. Then she drew a deep breath and smiled back at him. "I'm sorry, Philly. All I meant was, you shouldn't be worrying about that sort of thing, about going blind and being old and in pain. Not at your age. It's not right."

Philip's father patted her hand. His long face was amused. He looked at Philip and said, slowly and clearly as if Philip was foreign, or deaf, "At least you can have a bit of fun now, Phil old love. Lots of things to see. Your first visit to London."

Maggie said brightly, "My first visit too, Philly! So you and I have a full schedule. The Tower, the Houses of Parliament, Madame Tussaud's, Buckingham Palace..." She waved her hands about, jangling her bracelets and laughing. "Oh, we're going to have such a great time together!"

"First things first, Maggie," Philip's father said. "Let him see the house first, settle in, see how he likes it."

He smiled at her but there was an odd note in his voice, Philip thought. Almost as if he were warning her.

The house was tall and thin, one of a row of tall and thin houses. Steep, narrow stairs—by the time Philip had reached the top floor where he was to sleep, the backs of his legs hurt and he was panting and puffing.

"Quite a climb, five floors up," his father said. "Worth it, though, for the view."

He pushed up the sash window of the attic room and they stepped out, over a high sill, to a balcony. The houses were flat and plain at the front, on the street, but at the back balconies jutted out; a narrow one behind the roof parapet where they were standing, and a wider one two floors down. Below, at ground level, little gardens ran down to a canal where a long, gaily painted boat was tied up to the tow path. The boat, and the tall trees that grew on the bank on the other side of the canal, were reflected in the brown water.

Philip's father said, "Look, you can see St Paul's. That dome, between the two tower blocks."

Philip looked at St Paul's, then down at the canal and the gardens. His father's garden had a patch of grass, a small pond, and a paved terrace furnished with a white iron table and chairs. There was a drop from the terrace to the canal but no fence, and that surprised Philip. People said, *safe as houses*, he thought, but none of these houses were safe. Anyone could scramble up from the canal into the gardens, or creep along the balconies that joined the whole row together. Not the pirates he had been frightened of when he was little, but robbers. *Thieves*, Philip thought. Thieves, with stocking masks over their faces.

The idea made him shiver.

"Cold?" His father said. "Well, it is turning chilly. Dark, too. Look at the lights coming on in the tower blocks. Hideous buildings in the day time, but at night they look really quite magical." He looked at Philip and smiled. "Fairy castles."

"Those towers are the wrong shape for a castle," Philip said.

"Yes, I suppose so. I forgot you were familiar with that kind of architecture."

Philip's father chuckled as if something amused him. They climbed back through the window into the attic where Maggie was unpacking Philip's bag and putting his clothes away in a cupboard. Except for the bed and a bookcase and a rug on the floor, the attic was empty. In fact the whole house seemed bare to Philip after the crowded comfort of his grandmother's apartment. None of the rooms he had peeped into on his way up the stairs had much furniture in them. He had seen a few soft, baggy chairs and low tables and a couple of big, pottery vases with dried flowers for decoration, but no pictures, no silver framed photographs, no pretty ornaments . . .

Maggie was watching him look round the attic. She said, "We haven't done too much in this room. We left it for you to fix as you want it. I thought we might go out tomorrow and buy some good posters."

It hardly seemed worth it, just for a week, but it was kind of her. Philip said, "Thank you, but it's really quite all right as it is. It's all very comfortable."

Maggie's face lit with pleasure. "You like the house do you, honey?"

She was *nice*, Philip thought. He wondered if he should warn her. Even if she didn't have much to steal, she would be frightened if someone came sneaking in, looking . . .

He said, "I like it very much. I like the canal and the view. But if it was my house I must say I'd be a bit worried by thinking of burglars."

His father and Maggie both laughed. Maggie said, "Oh Philly! You are a dear, funny boy!"

It confused him a little, the way they kept laughing at him. His grandmother never laughed, unless he said something funny.

He wanted to telephone her when he had washed and come down to the kitchen for supper, but his father said he had already rung. He told Philip his grandmother had sent him her love and said she was going to bed.

"It's early for her," Philip said. "She's usually a bit of a night owl. I hope she's not lonely. I've never been away before except when I had my tonsils out in the hospital. I hope she's had something to eat. She'll only get a pain later on if she hasn't."

"For God's sake don't fuss, Phil," his father said. His voice was sharp and dry. "You sound like an old woman yourself."

Philip felt his ears start to burn. Maggie turned from the stove and laughed softly. She said, "Henry, honey! Hush now, my darling, it's sweet of him to think of his granny! How do you like your steak, Philly?"

"Cooked through," Philip said promptly. "Not bloody."

He hoped this didn't sound fussy, too. He remembered his grandmother's advice and found she was right. If he thought of a sheep's eye on his plate, cold and glistening and wobbly as jelly, even a raw steak didn't seem quite so dreadful. He said, "Though I really don't mind *all* that much. I mean, I really eat almost anything."

The dining room was part of the kitchen. They sat at a long, scrubbed, pine table and looked out at the garden through a glass door. There were candles on the table; their tiny, wavering flames, and the door and the dark garden beyond it were reflected in a gilt mirror that hung on the wall. They ate the steak with baked potatoes and salad, and there was apple pie afterwards.

"You must tell me what you like to eat, Philly, and I'll fix it for you," Maggie said. "I'm used to boys. I've got three pesky young brothers back home in Virginia. They used to be mad about baseball but this last year it's been soccer and skate-boards. Do you have a skate-board?"

Her dark hair and dark eyes and white teeth shone in the candle light. Philip's father watched her with a warm, smiling expression and when she smiled back at him it was as if private messages were passing between them. But now she was smiling at Philip.

He said, "I don't have a skate-board. My friend, William Morris has one, but my grandmother says the man who invented them ought to be shot because they're so dangerous. Not so much for the persons who use them, but for all the old people who can't get out of the way. Lady Anstruther almost had a bad fall last week because of a boy on a skate-board, she was quite shaken up when she came in to tell us, though she got better when we gave her a hot whisky toddy."

He was going to tell them more about Lady Anstruther; how she liked a 'little nip' now and then to oil her stiff joints, and how she missed her dead husband who had been an Air Marshal, but they seemed more interested in William Morris.

"Is he your best friend?" Maggie asked.

"He used to be," Philip said. "He still is, at school. But I

27

don't see him much afterwards, now he's got his skate-board."

"That's a shame," Maggie said.

"Not really. I mean, I was sorry to start with but I was getting bored with him anyway. Hanging around all the time and always wanting to come and have tea with grand-mother and me. It wasn't so bad in the winter, though he's not much good at backgammon, but now the light evenings are coming he'd get in the way when we go looking for bottles."

"Bottles?" Maggie said. "What kind of bottles?"

"Ones with messages in them from people stranded on desert islands. I used to think we might actually find one, and tell the Air Force to send a helicopter, and the Queen would give us a medal, though of course I don't think that now. I mean, I'm too old. But it's fun pretending and looking. And my grandmother enjoys it."

It sounded silly suddenly. As if this game his grandmother had invented to please him when he was little was one he only played now to please *her*. Well, not to please her, exactly, but because she still seemed to think that he believed in it.

Working this out made him feel muddled and tired. He was worn out, he decided, with being polite for so long. He yawned and said, "If you don't mind, I think I'm ready for bed. Thank you for a lovely supper."

Up in the attic he took off his best suit and hung it up carefully, put on his pyjamas and brushed his teeth at the wash basin. Then he knelt down by the bed for his prayers. He had just finished "Our Father", when Maggie came in. She waited just inside the door while he said his last prayer, the one his grandmother had taught him to make him feel safe when he had been frightened of pirates invading the castle. "Now I lay me down to sleep, I pray the Lord my soul to keep. And if I die before I wake, I pray the Lord my soul to take."

When he had finished and had got into bed, Maggie gave a funny, shy laugh and said, "Goodness, Philly! How spooky!"

He supposed that she meant it was scary to think about dying. He wondered if she were a heathen but it seemed rude to ask that. Red Indians probably had a different religion. He said, "Don't you pray at night, Maggie?"

"I'm afraid I don't, Philly." The blood rose in her cheeks and she came and sat on his bed, looking solemn. She said slowly, watching him with that solemn look, "If you're frightened of burglars, I can always lock up the window."

"It's all right," he said. "I'm not frightened."

"Oh," she said. "Good."

She leaned forward and kissed him. Her face and lips felt different from his grandmother's; smooth and firm instead of soft and baggy. When his grandmother kissed him, the stiff hairs round her mouth pricked him.

It was mean to remember that, he thought. His grandmother couldn't help being hairy. He sighed, and Maggie's arms tightened round him. She said, "Sleep tight, my honey."

He must have slept very deeply because when he first woke he couldn't think where he was. Darkness pressing all round him and a terrible noise in his ears; a wild wailing. Then he came fully awake and knew he was in his father's house, in the attic, and outside a siren was

29

screaming. An ambulance, or a fire engine, or a police car.

He got out of bed and went to the window. By the time he had pushed up the bottom sash and climbed over the sill to the balcony, the siren had died away and there was no sound except the soft hushing of the trees on the canal banks beneath him. The wind cooled his warm, sleepy face as he leaned on the parapet and looked out over London.

He couldn't see St Paul's now, there was too much cloud, but the tower blocks were still lit, and some of the windows in the row of houses in the street on the far side of the canal. As he watched, more lights came on in these windows, and he could see people moving about in the rooms. He wondered if the noisy siren had woken them too, or if they were people who always went to work early; office cleaners and postmen and newspaper boys. He could see a woman getting dressed, putting on her blouse and brushing her hair in a mirror, and two floors down, in the same house, a man was stretching his arms above his head, then bending, doing some exercise. It was rather exciting, Philip thought. He could see them, but they couldn't see him. It was like watching a play in a theatre.

He shivered and yawned, but although he was cold, he didn't feel tired, he decided. If he put on his jeans and his sweater, he would be warm enough. It was something his grandmother would enjoy doing, he thought; watching the people and making up stories about them. Something interesting he would be able to tell her when he got home; how he had perched up here, quiet and unseen on the roof-top, and watched all these people wake up. Like a spy, he thought, or a policeman, keeping an eye on the city.

Chapter 3

The robber came up from the canal and into the garden at daybreak. The first pale rays of the sun winked in the top windows of the houses opposite but the canal was still in deep shadow. From his high balcony, and in the blue, secret, dawn light, all Philip could see was a dark and spidery figure; long, thin arms clutching at the swaying branches of the weeping cherry tree that hung over the tow path, and long, thin legs swinging sideways on to the little paved terrace.

Philip ducked down behind the roof parapet. Although he felt a bit shaky as he dropped back through the window into his attic, he was more triumphant than frightened. Last night, his father and Maggie had laughed at him, hadn't they? As if they thought it was stupid to think about burglars! Well, they wouldn't laugh now!

Philip smiled to himself as he ran down the top flight of stairs to wake them up and tell them there was a thief in the garden, but outside their closed bedroom door he felt suddenly shy and went into the bathroom instead, to check that the thief was still there.

He had a closer view from the bathroom window than from outside his attic. The robber was crouching down on the terrace by the fish pond. He had a stick in his hand and seemed to be stirring the water. Philip wondered what he was doing. Robbers had bags of tools, didn't they? Not just sticks, but jemmies and spanners. Then, as Philip squashed the tip of his nose against the glass of the window, this robber looked up and Philip saw it was only a boy . . .

Philip was sure the boy hadn't seen him; he had moved away from the window too quickly. Holding his breath with excitement, he ran the rest of the way down the stairs, past the drawing room, past his father's study, down to the bottom of the tall house. He went into the kitchen and watched the boy through the glass of the garden door for a second, then gently unfastened the locks. The door creaked as he opened it but the boy didn't look up until Philip stepped into the garden and said, "What are you doing here?"

The Robbers

Although he meant to sound fierce, his voice came out thin and squeaky and the boy stood up, grinning, the dripping stick in his hand.

"I might ask you that," he said calmly. "I didn't know there was a kid here. Just that television man and his wife. Old Henry Holbein."

Philip said, "Henry Holbein's my father. I'm Philip Holbein," and then felt annoyed. Why should *he* have to explain? He said, speaking boldly and loudly now, because although the boy was taller and bigger than he was, he didn't look very much older, "You haven't answered my question!"

The boy shrugged his shoulders. "Just looking for tadpoles."

"Tadpoles?"

"Well, spawn. Frog spawn."

"So you *are* a thief, then!" Philip was surprised, because the boy didn't look like a robber. He didn't look guilty.

The boy laughed. He had a cheerful, freckled face and long, curling, red hair.

Philip said, "Nothing to laugh about. You go to Hell, stealing."

"No such place, dummy," the boy said, with scorn. "Besides, frog spawn's not stealing. It don't belong to no one. I mean, frog spawn is Nature."

"It's our pond, though," Philip said

"A pond is just water. No one owns water. Rain, and that. Still, if that's how you feel . . ." The boy gave an amused, lop-sided smile and picked up a jam jar from the terrace beside him. He said, "I'll be off, then."

B   33

"Oh," Philip said. It was only seven o'clock; a long time until breakfast, no one to talk to and nothing to do. He said, "It's all right. If you just want some spawn. I don't suppose my father would mind. I mean, I can give you permission."

"I've gone off the idea." The boy looked at him, smiling properly now, a happy, wide, friendly smile. "That's a lie, really. I've looked and there ain't any spawn, anyway. Looks as if the frogs have gone somewhere different this year."

"You've been here before then?"

The boy nodded. "House has been empty a long time. I used to get up in the garden to look at the pond. I never did no harm, like. I never lit fires, or anything."

"How did you know my father had bought it?"

"I live here, don't I?" He waved his hand vaguely towards the steep bank on the other side of the canal. From where they stood, in the garden, the trees on the bank, coming into spring leaf, hid the houses beyond them; the houses Philip had watched from his balcony.

He said, "Which house? I mean, I know we can't see from here, but I can see from the top of my house."

"We've got a green door," the boy said. "Needs a coat of paint, but you can still see it's meant to be green."

Excitement bubbled up inside Philip. "Can you get out on your roof? I was up on mine, outside the attic this morning. We could send signals. Morse code, with mirrors! Can you do the Morse code? What's your name?"

"Darcy Jones," the boy said. His eyes, green as a cat's, shone with laughter. "And I can't get up on my roof. We've

34

just got the ground floor and the basement. There used to be tenants up top, but they've gone. They're trying to get us out, too. Lousy bastards."

"What do you mean, *get you out*?"

Darcy shook his head. "Never mind . . ." He squatted on the edge of the terrace, caught hold of a cherry tree branch, and swung down to the tow path.

Philip looked at the drop. About eight feet, he thought. Taller than a tall man. "Wait a minute," he said, getting his courage together.

"Don't just jump, not from standing, you'll hurt your feet," Darcy Jones said. "Crouch down, like I did. But you ought to lock the back door first, if your Dad is still sleeping. In case someone gets in."

"My father isn't worried about that sort of thing," Philip said. He sat on the terrace with his legs dangling over the edge. He wriggled his bottom forward, grabbed at the tree, and missed. "More of a fall than a jump," he said as he reached the ground, sprawling.

"Takes practice," Darcy said, picking him up. "All right, are you?"

"Torn my jeans, I think," Philip said, feeling behind him. He looked at the boat that was tied up to the tow path. It was bright with paint and brass fittings and the windows were curtained. Perhaps people were sleeping inside. "Does someone live there?" he whispered. "Why is it so long and so narrow? I've never seen such a narrow boat."

"That's what it's called," Darcy said. "Narrow boat. Made to go through the canal tunnels. Like that tunnel up there."

Philip looked where he pointed, at the dark, low mouth of the tunnel that went under the road at the end of the terrace of houses.

Darcy said, "That one's a mile long. In the old days, they used these narrow boats to carry coal and things. They had horses to pull them along except when they went through the tunnels, then the boatman had to send the horse over the top and walk the boat through, like. Lying on his back with his feet on the roof of the tunnel. Only they've got engines now, and most of the boats are used just for holidays. This one's the Church Club boat. They take kids on trips at weekends."

"You know a lot don't you?" Philip said.

Darcy looked at him sharply. "You being funny?"

Philip was surprised by his tone. "No," he said. "Why? Did I sound funny? I didn't mean to. I mean, I like being told things."

"Oh. That's all right, then." For some reason, Darcy laughed loudly. He gave Philip a friendly shove and said, "Come on, let's get going. I'll show you the lock if you like."

There was the tunnel at one end of this stretch of the tow path and a bridge at the other. As they walked under the dark arch of the bridge icy droplets of water fell on Philip's head and trickled down, through his hair, to his nose. He stuck out his tongue to taste the drips and laughed happily. London was turning out much more interesting than he had expected. He had made a friend, and the canal was lovely, with the trees and the houses reflected in it, and ducks swimming, and little black fish that flashed silver when the sun touched them.

"Just coarse fish," Darcy said. "Perch and that. My Dad says there used to be trout in the old days but the water's too dirty now. People chucking in rubbish."

There was certainly a lot of rubbish at the lock. The white water rushing down the sluice at the side looked clean and sparkly but where it was trapped against the closed gates it was slimy green and cluttered with garbage; squashed beer cans, empty bottles and old plastic bags. There was even a dead dog, floating belly up, just under the surface. Philip said, "*Yukky.*"

"My Dad says people who chuck litter into the water ought to be shot," Darcy said.

Philip laughed again. "My grandmother is always saying people who do things she doesn't like ought to be shot. Has your father ever shot anyone? Is he a soldier?"

"He used to be a lock-keeper," Darcy said. "We had that cottage over there, at the end, by the basin. But he had to give up the job when he got crippled up with the rheumatism. Then we had to go and live with my brother and his wife, Addie, and my Mum got fed up, and went off."

Philip wondered where she had gone, but was too shy to ask. He looked shyly at Darcy. "My mother's dead."

"Mine might as well be," Darcy said. "Silly cow."

He whistled under his breath; then glanced sideways at Philip. "Tell you what. I've got to go back now, to see to my Dad. Addie gets him his breakfast but he needs a bit of help after, when she goes off to work. You can come too, if you want. He watches television a lot, my Dad does, and he thinks the world of your Dad. So he'd be interested to meet you." He hesitated. "If you've got time, like. I mean, you don't have to."

His face had flushed crimson. Philip said, "But I'd *love* to!"

He skipped beside Darcy, up the steps by the side of the canal bridge. Excitement was making his head buzz. He stopped in the middle of the bridge and looked down at the tall terrace of houses mirrored in the still water. He threw a stone and the reflection broke into shivery pieces. He said, "I feel really quite *fizzy*."

"Mugwump," Darcy said.

"That's a good word."

"It's what my Dad calls me sometimes," Darcy said.

Over the bridge, they turned into Darcy's street. His house was halfway along; the green door was open and a tall, handsome black woman stood on the front step, looking out. She was wearing a red coat and red boots. She said, "There you are, Darcy! Keeping me waiting!"

"I got held up," Darcy said. "Sorry, Addie. You won't be late, will you?"

"No. It's just that I like to be early. That Mrs Trumpeter always has her eye on the clock. Not that I blame her. After all, I get paid by the hour. Who's your friend?"

She smiled at Philip; a lovely, warm, welcoming smile. He smiled back at her. She was very pretty, with her smooth, shining, black skin, and her soft mop of dark hair, but her smile made her beautiful.

Darcy said, "This is Philip. He lives in one of them houses opposite."

"One of *those* houses," Addie corrected him. "Don't they

38

teach you anything, at that school?" She shook hands with Philip. "I'm Adelaide Jones," she said. "Darcy's sister-in-law. I'm sorry I can't stop, but he'll give you a cup of tea, and perhaps we'll meet later."

She was like a Queen, Philip thought, or a Duchess. So gracious and proud. He watched her as she walked down the street, holding her head steady and high as if she were used to wearing a crown, and said, "Who's Mrs Trumpeter?"

"Old bag she works for," Darcy said. "Lazy tart can't scrub her own floors. Come on in, Dad'll be fretting."

Although the house was shabby outside, peeling paint and cracked steps, inside it was clean as a palace: white walls and floor boards gleaming with polish. Through an open door, Philip saw a piano. He said, "Do you play, Darcy?"

"A bit. But that's Addie's piano. She and Bing live on this floor. Dad and me, we're in the basement so Dad can get out in the garden."

He clattered ahead down the stairs and opened a door into a big room, full of green light. Like an underwater cave, was Philip's first thought, but it was really more like a greenhouse. Hot, and smelling of earth, and plants everywhere; outside in the tiny, back garden, and inside in pots, clambering up the walls, even over the ceiling. Plants with thick, shining, green leaves; plants with long, spotted tongues; flowering plants with delicate petals. And, in the middle, in a clearing in this jungle, a huge television set and an old man in a brass bed, hunched against pillows.

Darcy said, "I couldn't get the tadpoles, Dad. But I've

brought Philip to see you. Philip Holbein. Henry Holbein's son."

"Henry Holbein's son is better than any old tadpoles," Mr Jones said. He held out a hand like a claw, with a leather strap and a splint. "How do you do, Philip Holbein? I'm pleased to meet you. I think a lot of your father."

He wasn't as old as he seemed, Philip realised. His fingers were shaky and swollen up at the knuckles but his voice and his eyes were much younger.

Philip said, "I'm sorry about your rheumatism, Mr Jones. Though it's arthritis, really, isn't it? My grandmother has some friends with arthritis and one of them, Lady Anstruther, wears a splint like yours sometimes."

"Lady Anstruther, eh? You mix with the aristocracy, do you, young Philip! Well, arthritis is no respecter of persons," Mr Jones said. He looked at his crooked hand. "I used to think, when I couldn't use this hand of mine to bang in a nail any longer, I would be happy to go. Shuffle off this mortal coil, as it says in Shakespeare. But, alas, the Lord didn't will it."

"Don't be morbid now, Dad," Darcy said. "Count your blessings. I'll pour your tea, shall I?"

Mr Jones closed his eyes. There was almost no flesh on the bones of his face and with his eyes closed his head looked like a skull. He said, "Adelaide is a blessing. I have two good sons and a daughter-in-law who is a pearl among women. No need to remind me, young Darcy. But I would like you to remember that I bear my pain alone!"

Philip thought that he sounded a little like Lady Anstruther in one of her miserable moods. He said, encouragingly, "You'll feel better when you've had a nice cup of tea."

"Three spoons of sugar, don't forget, Darcy," Mr Jones said. He opened his eyes, which were sharp and green as his son's, and smiled at Philip quite cheerfully. "Television is another blessing, young man. I may be an old cripple but I like to keep in touch with the world and your father helps me do that, more than most. He's a fine man. A lot of what I hear I take with a good pinch of salt, but if Henry Holbein says something, I always believe it. You might tell him that, Philip. It's my honest opinion."

"I'll tell him," Philip said. "I'm sure he'll be interested."

He watched while Darcy gave his father a mug of tea and tucked a napkin under his chin. Mr Jones managed the mug quite well, Philip noticed, and, when he had finished his tea, ate a thick slice of brown bread and marmalade.

It was good marmalade, with fat chunks of rind, and the bread was good, too, with a faintly sour, pleasant taste. Philip had several slices and, while he was eating, a good idea came to him. If Mr Jones was pleased to see him, because he was Henry Holbein's son, he would be even more pleased to see Henry Holbein! He helped Darcy carry the dirty dishes to a sink under the stairs and said, speaking quietly because they had left the door open, "Does your father ever go out?"

"In the garden when it's warm enough," Darcy said. "And sometimes down to the pub in the wheelchair when Bing's not too busy."

"What's Bing's job?"

"Antiques. He's a dealer. Old silver and stuff. He's got a stall up the road in the Market. Tuesdays and Saturdays."

"Perhaps my father would come here to see your Dad," Philip whispered. "At least, I could ask him."

"Wouldn't bother, if I were you," Darcy said.

"Why? I mean, my father might like to meet someone who was such a keen fan, and he'd like to see the room, too. All those plants!"

Bending over the sink, holding the mugs under the running tap, Darcy shook his head. He had gone rather pink.

Philip said, "It won't hurt to *ask*."

"Might hurt *me*, though." Darcy turned the tap off, looked at Philip, and sighed. "It's like they say in the shops to stop people asking for credit. A refusal often offends."

"I don't understand," Philip said.

"You don't know much, do you?"

"Perhaps I don't," Philip said. "But when I said that you *did*, that you knew a *lot*, you were angry!"

He was relieved to see Darcy smile. Darcy said, "Oh, all right, mugwump! Your Dad is important, mine isn't. He's just a grouchy old man. I don't want your Dad coming here out of charity. That's all I meant, really."

He left the mugs and plates draining and wiped the sink with a cloth. He said, "I've got to see to him, now. Help him to the toilet, and that. And you'd better get off. Your Dad don't know where you are, he'll most likely be worried."

Philip's father wasn't worried. He was angry. Philip ran home the street way and rang the front door bell and when his father opened it, he was red-faced and tight-mouthed.

He said nothing until he had hustled Philip down the stairs to the kitchen. Then he started to shout. Philip had behaved shockingly. He had gone out without telling them. He had left the garden door unlocked. He had upset Maggie. She was "out of her mind with anxiety". She thought Philip had run away. They had been just about to ring up the police station!

"I'm sorry," Philip said. "I'm sorry. *I'm sorry.*"

He glared at his father. His father stopped shouting.

Maggie said, "Henry, honey! You'll frighten the child!"

"I'm not frightened," Philip said, truthfully—and then saw that she was. Standing by the stove, wide eyes alarmed, twiddling the end of her long braid in her fingers.

He said, speaking to her, deliberately ignoring his father, "It was just that I got up so early. You were asleep. And I went—well, I went into the garden to look at the canal, and I met a friend . . ."

"What friend?" his father said.

"This boy," Philip said. "I'm trying to *tell* you. We got talking, and he told me about the narrow boats, and the tunnels, and how they used to push the boats through with their feet in the old days, and then we went to the lock. We had a good time." He felt forlorn and furious. He said, "It's spoiled now, with this stupid fuss!"

"No," Maggie said. "Philly, dear, I'm glad you enjoyed yourself. It was simply that I was worried and that worried your father. If you'd just leave a note, another time. You must be hungry now. Would you like eggs and bacon?"

Philip was full up with brown bread and marmalade. But he nodded, to please her. "I really am sorry, Maggie," he said, meaning it this time. "I won't upset you again. I'll be good for the rest of this week."

"Why only this week?" his father asked. He sounded amused now, looking down his big nose at Philip, and smiling. "I hope you can manage to be good for a bit longer than that."

"Well, of course I can," Philip said. "I just meant, while I'm here. I'm always good at home."

"This is your home," his father said.

Philip looked at him. There was a long silence.

Maggie said, "Henry. Henry—I don't think she's told him!"

Although Philip heard this, it was as if he only heard it with his ears, not his mind. He said, reasonably, "I know it's my home, in a way. I mean, you're my father, and Maggie's my stepmother. But I *live* with my grandmother."

His father and Maggie were watching him with such solemn expressions! He said, frantically now, "I mean, I *have* to live with her, don't I? I have to go to *school*."

"Perfectly good school down the road," his father said. "Bit rougher, I daresay, than you have been used to, it's hardly a private academy for little gentlemen, but that won't hurt, will it? Do you good, I should think. Knock a few corners off. You didn't really expect to live in that bloody castle for the rest of your life, did you, Philip? Not now Maggie and I can look after you. After all, your grandmother's old. An old woman."

Philip said nothing. There was nothing to say. His father cleared his throat and said, much more gently, "Phil old love, she did explain, didn't she?"

Philip's throat was hot. He swallowed, to cool it, and said, "Yes, she did tell me, of course. I just hoped that she didn't mean it."

44

He bottled his anger up. He was polite, he was good, he ate what they gave him and did what they said. They took him to the Tower of London and he listened to all that they told him about it and thanked them for telling him. He said, "That was very interesting." When they came back to the house, in the late afternoon, they suggested a walk along the canal and he said he was tired and would rather watch television. They went out without him and the moment the door closed he ran to the telephone.

As soon as his grandmother answered, he said, "Do you know where I've been today? To the Tower! I've seen Traitor's Gate! Do you know what they used to do with traitors in the old days? They used to cut their heads off and stick them on spikes!"

His grandmother said, "I'm sorry, Philip. I should have told you."

"I told them you *did*! I didn't let you down! I told a lie for you. You made me tell them a *lie*!"

"Only a white lie," his grandmother said.

Her voice sounded thin and tired, but it didn't make him sorry for her. It made him angrier still.

"How could you?" he raged. "If you'd told me I'd got to stay, I'd never have *come*. Not unless they'd dragged me here, screaming. You knew that, didn't you? That's why you cheated! Pretending it was just for a holiday! That was so *mean*! Why did you do it? Did you want to get rid of me?"

"That's unkind," his grandmother said.

"I don't care! Is it *true*?"

If it was true, he thought, he wouldn't bother her ever

45

again. He would kill himself! Or go right away somewhere, find a place to hide where no one could find him . . .

His grandmother said, sounding stronger and firmer now, "Of course I didn't want to get rid of you. But I had no choice, Philip. He is your father."

"I didn't think he was my brother, did I? What's his being my *father* got to do with it? He hasn't looked after me, ever."

"Only because he couldn't. Not because he didn't want to. Now things are different. He's got a wife. You're older. I'm older."

"He keeps on about that! As if you were falling apart!"

His grandmother laughed. "Oh, he would! Now it suits him!"

Philip said, "He didn't think you were too old until he got married, did he? And I don't think he *does* want me, really. I think it's Maggie who's made him think that he ought to."

"Oh, Philip," his grandmother said.

"Is that one of the things I'm allowed to think, but not say?"

She didn't answer this. But her silence had answered him. He grinned to himself, and went on, "It's silly, all this talk about ages. I met a boy this morning and his father's much younger than you but he's all crippled up with arthritis. That's being old. Not just birthdays. You're not old to *me*. I want to come home, grandmother. I could. I could just run away and come home."

"I should send you back at once, make no mistake! And your father would be angry with both of us. You might not mind that, but I would."

46

"Blackmail,' Philip said. "You're blackmailing me."

She sighed, "Give your father a chance."

"What kind of chance?"

"A term, Philip. A term at this school that he wants you to go to. Then you can come and stay here in the summer and we'll discuss it again."

He knew, by her carefully calm, level tone, that this had not been her idea. It was what his father had decided, and she had agreed, because his father had made her. She might not be too old for some things, like playing backgammon and looking for bottles with messages in them, but she was too old to fight with his father. Too old to win, anyway. *She* was too old, and *he* was too young, Philip thought. He said, "All right, then. I suppose I'll get used to it." And realised, as he said this, that he was getting used to it already.

"Thank you," his grandmother said. "Thank you, Philip."

He wondered what she was thanking him for. After all, he'd done nothing. Then she said, sounding shaky, "You're a brave boy, a good soldier, just like your grandfather," and he felt ashamed suddenly. Although it was nice to be praised, he didn't deserve it because although he felt a bit sad, he wasn't feeling as sad as she seemed to think he must be. But he couldn't say that. It might hurt her. So all he said was, "I shall miss you, grandmother."

Chapter 4

Philip kept watch on Darcy's green door from his attic balcony. Several times, over the Easter weekend, he saw Adelaide Jones come in or go out, but he didn't see Darcy. And although he walked down the street twice, slowing down outside the house and whistling, he was too shy to ring the bell. The more he thought about it, the more afraid he became that Darcy had been really offended when he had suggested that his father should visit poor Mr Jones. "Charity" Darcy had called it, and Philip remembered what

48

his grandmother had once said about charity. "A stone in the mouth to proud people."

On Tuesday morning, his father and Maggie took him to the Antique Market. Stalls, set up in a maze of paved alleys, sold old silver and china and glass. Old clothes, too; embroidered silk shawls and tattered lace blouses and petticoats, and ancient fur coats. It was a cheerful place, noisy and bustling. "Watch out for your purse, darling," Philip's father warned Maggie as they pushed their way through the crowd. "This place is a good hunting ground for pickpockets."

Maggie stopped at a stall to look at some plates with birds painted on them. She said, "Oh Henry, just look! These are so *pretty!*"

"Genuine Rockingham," the man behind the stall said. "You've got a bargain there, lady."

Philip's father put a monocle in his right eye, picked up a plate and examined it carefully. He let the monocle fall and said, "Rockingham? Really!" And laughed in a loud, incredulous way, to show that he didn't believe it. Philip was shocked. "Never be rude to shopkeepers or people who can't answer back," was a strict rule his grandmother had taught him. Embarrassed by his father's behaviour, he looked at the other things on the stall, little silver boxes, and sets of spoons and forks tied up in bundles, and cut glass decanters, and pretended to be interested in them while Maggie persuaded his father to buy the plates and his father haggled over the price and finally sighed and got out his cheque book.

"Bing Jones," the stall keeper said, when Philip's father

asked what name he should write on the cheque, and Philip was so startled that he almost dropped the silver box he was holding.

"Careful, sonny," Bing Jones said, and winked at him, grinning.

Philip stared. Bing was bigger and older than Darcy, of course, but he had the same freckly nose and wide grin and red hair. Philip smiled back as he put the box down. He wanted to say, "I know your brother," but it hardly seemed a good moment, since his father had been so rude to him.

"Did you really think Mr Jones was lying?" he asked, as they walked home.

"Lying?" his father said.

"About the plates being—well—whatever he said they were."

"Rockingham. I didn't say he was lying, did I?"

"Not in words. But you laughed."

"Oh, that's part of the game," his father said. "I'm not much of a judge, but they're probably genuine. He knew that I knew that! *And* that I knew why they were going so cheap. A good bargain that fell off the back of a lorry!"

"They can't have done that," Philip said. "I mean, if they had, they'd be broken."

His father and Maggie laughed at him then, but he didn't mind. He was getting used to the fact that they usually laughed when he didn't understand something, and simply waited for them to explain it. But when his father said that "falling off a lorry" meant stolen goods, he still felt confused. He said, "But if you knew they were stolen, you shouldn't have bought them, should you? You ought to have gone to the police."

Maggie laughed—but at his father, this time. They were in the house now, in the kitchen, and she was taking the bird plates out of their newspaper wrappings and setting them carefully down on the table. She said, "Out of the mouths of babes, Henry honey."

Philip's father said, rather quickly, "That's a point, Phil old love. But of course I couldn't *know* they were stolen, could I? It was just a guess because he was asking such a low price for them. It's not the same thing."

It didn't seem very different to Philip. But he didn't say so. He knew by the guarded tone of his father's voice, and the way his long nose had flushed red, that he mustn't argue.

He was learning quite fast when he could say what he thought and when it was best to keep quiet. His grandmother had been wrong about some things. She had been wrong about food. Although his father said that he mustn't have too much ice-cream or sweet things because they were bad for his teeth, he was never expected to eat fish or anything else that disgusted him. In fact, quite the opposite. Maggie said, "Just tell me what you like, Philly darling, and I'll cook it for you." But when, because she was being so nice, he told her what his grandmother had said about eating everything, even sheep's eyes, she was hurt. She said, "Oh, Philly, did she really think I would be such a horrible stepmother?" and he knew he should have kept his mouth shut.

He kept his mouth shut about school. When they asked him about it at the end of the first day, he said, "It's all right."

It *had* been all right in the morning. There were more boys and girls in his class than he was used to, and the noise they made, banging their desk lids and whispering while the teacher was talking, was rather distracting, but he got an A in a Maths test and enjoyed writing an essay on *My Favourite Place*. The teacher, whose name was Miss Tombs, read the class essays while they had an art lesson, and handed them back at the end of the morning. She was a big, muscular lady with thick glasses and large teeth that flashed white when she smiled. She flashed these white teeth at Philip as she gave him his essay and said, "That was extremely good, Philip. Very imaginative. I could almost believe that you really did know what it was like to live in a castle."

"Oh, but I do," Philip said. "I mean, I do live in a castle, when I'm at home with my grandmother." He explained about the Queen, and the Grace and Favour Apartment, and Miss Tombs smiled again, showing rather less of her teeth this time, and said, "Well, we'll have to call you Prince Philip, won't we?"

It had been a mistake to tell her the truth, Philip realised, when school dinner was over and they went into the playground. No one was nasty to him, just a few of the girls tittered and nudged each other and called him "Prince Philip", but it made him feel silly. He laughed to show that he didn't mind and after a while they got bored and left him alone. He wandered about in the playground, hoping that someone would ask him to join in a game, and when no one did, went and hid in the lavatories. He stayed there until the bell went for afternoon school. When he came out the cloakroom was empty but outside, in the corridor, two boys were leaning against the tiled wall, a fat boy and a thin boy. The fat boy stuck out a foot as Philip went past and Philip tripped over it. The fat boy doubled up, laughing. "I'm so *sorry*, your Majesty!"

Philip picked himself up. He said, "That's a stupid and boring joke. You must be a stupid and ignorant clod to think that it's funny."

He stuck his nose in the air and stalked off. They giggled behind him and when Philip looked over his shoulder the thin boy wiggled his hips and minced along on his toes, saying in a high, prim, wobbly voice, mimicking Philip, "Stupid and ignorant clod, stupid and ignorant clod." They caught Philip up as he reached the classroom and the fat boy punched him so hard in the back that he fell against Miss Tombs who was going through the door just in front of him. She turned sharply, looked down at Philip, then beyond him, at the fat boy. She was very alarming when she wasn't smiling; eyes rolling behind her thick spectacles, showing the whites, and mouth clamped tight over her teeth. Like an angry horse, Philip thought.

She said, before he could apologise to her, "That's enough, Adam Skinner! I warned you last term, but in case you've forgotten, I'm warning you again now. You may not be capable of learning much from me, no one can make bricks without straw, but I will not have rude and disruptive behaviour. And that goes for you, too, Moses Green. Just remember, I've got my eyes on the pair of you!"

Philip slipped past while she spoke to them, and sat down, hands neatly folded on the desk in front of him as he had been taught at his old school. As the two boys walked by his desk, the thin boy, Moses Green, stuck out his tongue, and the fat boy, Adam Skinner, scowled sullenly. They sat two rows behind Philip and for the rest of the afternoon, whenever Philip glanced back, Moses Green wrinkled his nose, pretending he smelled something bad, and Adam Skinner gave him a menacing glare. His eyes were small, dark, shiny buttons sunk in solid, red cushions of flesh. He was a bully, Philip thought, and his thin friend was a joker. A Joker and a Bully made a dangerous pair. He would have to watch out for them.

"Have you made any friends, Philip honey?" Maggie asked him.

"Oh, lots," Philip said. And, to distract her, "It's funny, our teacher's name is Miss Tombs, and she's got great, long, white teeth, just like tombstones."

Maggie laughed. "You must bring some of your friends home, Philly. Ask them to tea."

"Oh, I will," Philip said.

He wondered who he could ask, to please her. The girl who shared his desk had been nice, showing him where things were kept and helping him fill out his time table, but he guessed that his father and Maggie would expect him to bring home a boy. And, so far, the boys in his class had ignored him.

They were afraid of Adam and Moses, Philip decided. Adam was stupid but strong and Moses was sharp and sarcastic and sneery. No one would dare to make friends with a new boy if the Bully and the Joker had chosen to pick on him, even if all they had done up to now was glare and pull silly faces. They would get tired of that, Philip told himself philosophically. As long as he lay low and kept out of their way they would get bored in the end.

He kept out of their way for three days. He was careful not to arrive at school until just before the bell rang, avoided the cloakroom unless there were other boys there, and kept a sharp look-out in the playground. Exploring round the back of the buildings, he found a gap in the high, iron railings that fenced off the canal, and when school was over, instead of leaving by the main entrance he escaped through this gap, squeezing through the bent rails and dropping down to the tow path.

This part of the canal, between the school and the lock, was silent and derelict. No fishermen, no barges, only a few ducks paddling the slow, dark, velvety water, and huge, empty factories with smashed windows lining the banks. Philip was a bit scared the first day as he ran home on the tow path, feeling the shattered windows of the old factories watching him like dead eyes, but as he grew bolder, he began to enjoy being the only person alive in this quiet, secret place. No one else dared to come here except Philip Holbein, the gallant explorer. "Come out, whoever you are!" he shouted at ghostly enemies lurking in the empty buildings, and his hollow voice echoed back from the high walls, making his flesh creep very pleasantly. He swaggered along, swishing the dusty nettles out of his way with a stick, ten feet tall and brave as a lion.

On the third day, his real enemies caught him. He didn't see them lying in wait; the sun was in his eyes as he ran past the lock and it was dark under the bridge where the Joker and the Bully were hiding. If Philip had not heard Moses Green's thin, giggly laugh just behind him, he would have had no warning at all; as it was, he only had time to spin round and face them before they dragged him under the black arch of the bridge and slammed him breathless against the cold, dripping wall. Adam held him there, pinned, arms spread and helpless and jabbed a knee in his stomach. Philip gasped and spat in Adam's face. Adam grinned. He said, "Dirty little boy, isn't he, Moses? What shall we do with him?"

Philip said, "Why should you do anything? I've done nothing to you." He tried to be Philip Holbein, the gallant explorer, faced with a savage tribe. He said, as haughtily as he could manage, "Let me go at once or you'll be in trouble."

"Oh, I don't think we can do that," Moses said. "Tell you what, though. We'll give you a choice. Would you rather have your ears twisted off, or your nose slit? I think my knife is just about sharp enough."

Adam laughed. His breath puffed sourly in Philip's face. He said, "Dunno as we ought to leave marks on him, Moses. Nasty little fink might go running to Teacher."

"Duck him in the canal, then," Moses said. "Make him drink it. That'll give him a belly ache he won't forget in a hurry."

Adam shifted his grasp and twisted Philip's right arm up behind him, forcing him down on his knees on the edge of the canal, pushing his head down. Philip saw a dead fish floating, silver and slimy, and twisted his face away. "There's worse than dead fish, Your Royal Highness," Moses said in a sepulchral voice. "There's corpses in there, dead men with no eyes."

"Please," Philip begged, "please don't, *please* . . ."—but Adam's hand pushed hard on the back of his neck and his face went down, into the water. He closed his eyes and held his breath until it seemed his lungs were bursting. They yanked his head up, by his hair, let him gulp air for a second, then shoved him down again. This time the water went up his nose and down his throat and he thought he was drowning. He wriggled and thrashed, and, when they let him go suddenly, nearly fell into the water. He grabbed the concrete side of the canal and pulled himself back to safety, choking and retching. Drums banged in his ears; then a loud, hollow slapping. When he had stopped being sick, he raised his head dizzily and saw that Moses had disappeared and that Adam was flat on his back on the tow path with someone kneeling on top of him and hitting him, open-handed, first on one side of his face and then on the other. Philip blinked. He said, "*Darcy!*" and got to his feet. He saw blood on Adam's face and his eyes open and staring. Philip said, terrified, "Darcy, *don't* . . ."

Darcy stopped hitting Adam. He stood up and kicked him. He said, "Get up, filthy slob."

Adam got up. Blood ran from his nose, down his chin. He smeared the blood over his face with the back of his hand and glared at Philip with his dark, button eyes. Philip shook. Darcy said, "Don't you take it out on him, Skinner. You touch him again and I'll cripple you."

Adam scowled. He turned and limped off. Philip said, "Thank you, Darcy. You saved my *life*. Really! I think they were going to *drown* me."

Darcy shrugged. "What made you get mixed up with them two?"

"I didn't. I mean, I didn't do anything. They just don't like me, I think. They're in my class at school."

"Old Miss Tombs? Old Horse Face?" Darcy laughed. "She was my teacher last year."

"I didn't know you were at that school. I haven't seen you."

"No. Well." Darcy laughed again, a bit awkwardly. "I've been a bit busy. Other things to do, like." He looked at Philip. "You're in a mess, ain't you?"

Philip sighed. His shirt was torn and his jacket was sodden. He thought that he didn't want to go back and face Maggie like this; admit he'd been beaten up. It was shameful, somehow. He took off his jacket and wrung out some of the water. He said, "Perhaps it'll dry out in the sun."

Darcy was watching him. "You scared to go home?"

"No." Philip flushed. "No, of course not."

"You can come to my place, if you like. Addie can put your things in the dryer. Long as you don't tell her I've been skiving off school. She'd be mad at me. Addie thinks a lot of education."

"I'm not sneaky," Philip said. "But you have to go to school, don't you? I mean, it's the law."

"Oh, the *law*!" Darcy said. "Lots of things is the *law*. Still, maybe I'll turn up tomorrow. Better had, hadn't I? Keep a bit of an eye on you!"

The sound of music met them as they went in. Addie was playing the piano and Mr Jones, sitting beside her in a wheel chair, was singing, *Oh hear us when we cry to Thee, For those in peril on the sea.*

Darcy rolled his eyes at Philip. He led him past the front room, down the passage to the kitchen. Philip removed his jacket and Darcy put it in the electric dryer. He turned the switch and said, "Dad likes a bit of a sing song. Especially when he's got a drink or two in him. Bing wheeled him down the pub lunch time."

Philip wondered why Darcy seemed so embarrassed. He said, "I like that hymn. And your father has a nice voice."

"Used to have," Darcy mumbled. He looked sideways at Philip. "He'd like it if you told him, though. Buck him up."

They went to the front room and stood by the piano. When the hymn was finished, Philip said, "You sing very well, Mr Jones."

Mr Jones looked pleased and patted his chest with his clawed-up fingers. "Not as much expansion here as there ought to be. I was a grand singer once, but that's gone to pot along with the rest of me. When troubles come, they come not single spies but in battalions. As the Bard says. I've handed on the torch to Darcy now. He's got the voice of the family. Good enough for the cathedral choir school, isn't he, Addie?"

"They'll only take him if he works hard at his lessons, too," Addie said. She looked at Darcy, a long, thoughtful look, as if she guessed he had been playing truant, and Darcy hung his head.

"I like singing," Philip said, to distract Addie's attention. "At home, I mean when I lived with my grandmother, we often sang hymns in the evening."

"Did you, my lovely?" Addie beamed at him. She had braided her woolly hair in thin, oiled strips, tight to her scalp, and it made her look different from the first time Philip had seen her, but just as beautiful.

"What shall we have, then?" Mr Jones said. His green eyes were sharp and excited and his thin cheeks were flushed. "What about, *To be a pilgrim*, Addie?" He hiccuped gently and said, "Pardon me."

"Oh, leave off, Dad," Darcy muttered. He glanced shyly at Philip.

Philip said, "That's one of my best favourites, Mr Jones. My grandmother likes it, too. She says it's a good soldier's song. My grandfather was a soldier, you see."

"*He who would valiant be, 'Gainst all disaster*," Mr Jones sang. Philip sang with him, Addie picked up the tune, and when they got to the lines, *Hobgoblin nor foul fiend, Shall daunt his spirit*, Darcy joined in, hesitantly at first, as if he felt nervous, singing in front of Philip, then his voice gathered strength and rose full and pure and sweet. "*He knows he at the end, Shall life inherit*," Darcy sang, and, catching Philip's eye, smiled at him happily.

After that they sang, *Immortal, invisible, God only wise*, and *Hark the herald angels sing*, and *All things bright and beautiful*. Singing these old hymns made Philip feel a little homesick for his grandmother, but it made him happy, too. Happy and sad at the same time. Then Addie put the piano lid down and swung round on the stool. "That's enough now," she said. "I've got to get tea. Bing will be home in a minute. Do you want to stay, Philip?"

"I'm sorry, I'd like to, but I'd better go home," Philip said. "But thank you. Thank you very much for the singing."

"A pleasure," Addie said. "A pleasure for me to hear children's voices praising the Lord. You must come again, chicken."

When she had gone to the kitchen, Mr Jones said, "Your grandfather was an officer, I suppose. A Captain, was he, young Philip?"

"Well, no, Mr Jones," Philip said. For some reason he felt reluctant to tell him the truth. Perhaps he was afraid Mr Jones would laugh at him as Miss Tombs had done when he said that he lived in a castle. But it seemed wrong to lie. As if he was ashamed of his grandfather. He said, "He was a General, Mr Jones, actually. But of course he's dead now."

"Well, we all come to it, both prince and peasant," Mr Jones said. This thought seemed to content him; he smiled, a small, secret smile, and said, "Mixing with the nobs, Darcy! Have to mind our manners, won't we?"

"Oh, *Dad*!" Darcy groaned, and, from behind his father's back, winked at Philip. "Come on," he said. "Get your jacket."

Philip's jacket was crumpled, but dry. Philip put it on and Darcy came to the front door with him. He said, "You mustn't mind my Dad."

"Oh, I don't," Philip said, although he wasn't quite sure what Darcy meant. He stood on the step, wondering if he dare ask Darcy to tea. Darcy might be bored. He was in a higher class than Philip. Even though he had saved him from

Adam and Moses, he might not want to be friends with a younger boy. In his mind, Philip heard his grandmother say, *Nothing venture, nothing win.*

He said, "Would you like to come to my house to tea? Tomorrow, or the next day? Maggie, my stepmother, keeps asking me to bring someone."

"Daresay I would," Darcy said. "Long as Bing don't want me to help him. Though that's usually mornings, of course." He lowered his voice. "Matter of fact, that's why I've not been to school. I've been helping him, sorting the stuff for the stall, and today we went down to the city, to the silver market. We got up at four and didn't get back till gone nine. Smashing fun, all in the dark to begin with, poking about in the backs of the lorries with torches."

"Lorries?" Philip said. He remembered what his father had told him about things falling off the back of a lorry and felt himself blushing. "I thought you said you went to a *market*."

"Well, that's what it is, ain't it? Just for dealers, like the fish and meat markets. Or Covent Garden for vegetables."

"Oh, I see."

"Perhaps you'd like to come some time," Darcy said casually.

"Oh, I'd *love* to."

"Course, I'd have to ask Bing. So I can't make any promises. Maybe your father wouldn't let you come, anyway."

Philip felt his cheeks growing hot again as he thought of the unkind things his father had said about Bing but he answered, stoutly, "Oh, I'm sure he would. Long as I pick the right moment to ask him."

Chapter 5

"Please God," Philip prayed. "Please, God, if You can manage it, could you make my father be out of the house when Darcy comes to tea? And, if that is too difficult, please don't let him say anything nasty about Bing in front of Darcy."

Philip's grandmother had told him that he should never ask for things for himself when he prayed, or only for important things, like knowing how to be good. He hoped, as he finished his prayer, that God would understand he was making this request for Darcy's sake, not for his own. Or only a little bit for his own. He wondered if he should point this out but decided that it might sound rather rude, as if he thought God wasn't smart enough to see it for himself. So all he said was, "I hope You don't mind my asking, but Darcy would be upset, even if my father only meant to make a joke."

His prayer was answered. His father wasn't there when Darcy turned up, wearing a clean white shirt and with his curly red hair tamed and darkened with water, and when he did come in, halfway through tea, he was in a good mood, smiling and friendly. He shook hands with Darcy and said he was pleased to meet him, and asked polite questions like where Darcy lived, and what his father did, and if Darcy had any brothers or sisters. Darcy answered equally politely, calling Philip's father "Sir", and explaining that his father used to be a lock-keeper on the canal but was retired now because of his rheumatism.

"Mr Jones watches television a lot," Philip said. "He watches your programmes. He thinks they are very good."

"Thank you," his father said. "I'm glad."

He smiled at Darcy who frowned and said quickly, changing the subject, "I've only got one brother, Sir. He's an antique dealer. Bing Jones. Everyone knows him round here. He's got a stall up the market."

Philip felt faint and sick, but his father only said, very pleasantly, "I think we know him, too. In fact, we bought some china from him the other day, didn't we, Maggie?"

"Lovely plates," Maggie said. "Really beautiful!" She blushed as she spoke, glancing at Philip's father, and Philip saw, with surprise, that she was as nervous as he was in case his father said something tactless. And then, by the way his father laughed and stretched out his hand to touch hers, that he understood how she was feeling and wanted to reassure her.

He said gravely, to Darcy, "You must tell your brother how pleased we have been with his plates. We will certainly look at his stall again, the next time we go to the market."

Darcy said, "Of course, the stall is just a beginning. I mean, my brother will get a proper shop when the business really gets going. Only there's a lot to be thought of. It's all right to think big, my brother says, but best not to *act* big until you've got something behind you."

"Very wise," Philip's father said. He was smiling a little, but it was a kind smile.

Darcy said, "Once Bing's got a year's rent saved up, he's going to see about the shop. Course, the bank would lend him the money, but my Dad's against that. He says, neither a borrower nor a lender be. That's from William Shakespeare. My Dad thinks a lot of Shakespeare. Though Bing says there weren't no proper banks to borrow from when Shakespeare was alive, so he couldn't really know, could he?"

"I suppose Shakespeare was thinking of borrowing from friends or from money lenders," Philip's father said. "I think that borrowing from a bank, nowadays, is a bit different."

"Bing won't go against my Dad," Darcy said.

"Won't he? Well. That's an unusual filial attitude," Philip's father said. But although he sounded amused, he was looking at Darcy with interest. As though he were really interested in him, not just being polite because he was Philip's friend, and it made Philip feel happy and proud.

Up in his room, after tea, he said, "My father likes you."

Darcy shrugged his shoulders.

Philip said, "I mean, of course Maggie does, too. It's just that my father is funny sometimes."

"I suppose being on television makes him think he's important," Darcy said. "Seemed all right to me, though. I like Maggie. Is she a Red Indian?"

"I don't know." Philip giggled. "Why don't you ask her?"

"Addie says it's rude to ask personal questions. She don't like it when people ask her. Where she comes from, and that. Just because she's black they think that she's foreign." He looked round the room. "Nice up here, ain't it? Private, like. Wish *I'd* got my own television!"

"Maggie bought it for me. She and my father don't like the same programmes as I do. I don't watch it much, really."

Philip thought it was dull, watching television alone, but he didn't say so. Since Darcy thought he was lucky to have his own set, it might seem like showing off.

He said, "Shall I put it on now?" It would be something to do.

Darcy shook his head. "Nothing on, is there? Just the kids' programmes." He stuck his hands in his pockets and yawned.

Philip's heart sank. Darcy was bored, as he had been afraid he would be. He said, "We could get out on the roof, if you like."

"I don't mind," Darcy said.

They climbed out of the window and stood on the balcony. "You can see St Paul's," Philip said. "And the Post Office Tower. And your house." He looked hopefully at Darcy but he was staring into space, frowning. Philip said, "Of course it's nicer when it's dark, really. With all the lights on in the windows. You can watch all the people."

"Mmm," Darcy said.

Philip sighed. "The balconies run along the whole row of houses. On this floor, and two floors down. You could walk right along."

"You'd get into trouble if someone saw you," Darcy said sternly. "Trespassing."

But he was looking more interested. Philip said, "You could *creep*. Like a burglar."

Darcy laughed. "Or that cat."

"What cat?"

"Can't you hear it?"

Philip listened. He heard a faint mewing.

"It's a kitten, I think," Darcy said. He called it. "Puss, puss . . ."

A little cat jumped over the wall that divided the balcony from the next house and wound itself round their ankles. It was black, except for one white paw, and wore a red collar.

"Poor little bugger!" Darcy bent down and stroked it. "Lost, are you?"

"Not very lost," Philip said. "It belongs to the old lady next door. I've seen it with her in the garden."

"It thinks it's lost, though," Darcy said. He picked up the

kitten and rubbed his chin against its soft body. "It's frightened. You can tell by the way the fur has gone stiff. I think it got out of that little window and doesn't know how to get back. Silly baby. Well, that's easy put right."

He stepped over the dividing wall. The house next door had a big window facing the canal, and a tiny one, high up in the wall at the side. This window was open. Darcy pushed the cat through it. He said, "There you are, pussy." But they could still hear it mewing.

Darcy looked through the big window. Philip joined him and saw that the room was the same shape as his own, with a sloping ceiling on the far side. There were brightly patterned rugs on the floor and a lot of heavy, dark, polished furniture.

"Door's shut, that's why it's crying," Darcy said. They watched it, scratching at the closed door. "Poor little sod," Darcy said, and, as if it had understood him, the kitten ran across the room to the window and looked up at them.

Darcy said, "If we could get in, we could open that door. This big window's locked but we could squeeze in through the small one." He stepped back and examined it. "I couldn't, I'm too big, but you might be able to. If you sort of wiggled your shoulders."

"That really would be trespassing," Philip said. "It'll be all right, Darcy. She'll hear it quite soon, the old lady."

"How d'you know?" Darcy said. "She might be deaf, or asleep. If she's old. It might be trapped there for *ages.*" His voice had gone husky suddenly and Philip saw there were tears in his eyes. Darcy turned his head away and said gruffly, "It's pitiful!"

Philip felt weak at the knees. He said, "I'll climb in, course I will. I'm not scared, Darcy!"

It was easier than he had expected to go up the sloping roof and into the window feet first. He squeezed his shoulders through, and dropped down. Inside the room he stood, listening, but all he could hear was his own, thumping heart. He crept across the room, making no sound on the rich carpets, and opened the door. The little cat darted out and fled down the stairs like a shadow. Philip closed the door gently and went back to the window. It was so high in the wall that it was going to be harder to get out than it had been to get in, even though Darcy was peering through, ready to help him. "I'll haul you up," Darcy offered, but Philip shook his head. He moved a chair and stood on it and put his outstretched arms and shoulders through the opening. Darcy tugged until Philip's stomach was on the sill, then the rest of him came out with a rush and they tumbled together down the roof, to the parapet.

Neither of them spoke until they were safely in Philip's attic. For a second they looked at each other, both red in the face, breathing hard. Darcy said, "*Good man!*" and then put his hand to his mouth as if he were startled by his own voice. He whispered, "Why did you shift that chair, though? Someone might notice."

"I'd have made dirty marks on the wall with my feet if I hadn't," Philip said. He felt tingly—pins and needles prickling all over him. He thought of something wonderfully funny to say, and he said it. "I'm a very *clean* burglar."

"You're a *cat* burglar," Darcy amended, which seemed funnier still. They both started to giggle. The giggles grew into laughter; they collapsed on the floor and rolled about, laughing, until they were both quite exhausted.

Darcy lay on his back and sighed. He looked at the ceiling and said, "I wouldn't have bothered, you know, if it hadn't been just a kitten. I mean, so little and scared. I don't care for cats all that much. I'd rather have a dog. Addie would get me one, only we aren't allowed to have dogs. We rent our place, see, and they don't allow animals, and Addie says they're just waiting for us to put a foot wrong. They can't turn us out unless they find somewhere else for us suitable, not as long as we pay the rent regular, but if we got a dog, they'd have an excuse. They'd put us out straight-away."

"Who's *they*?" Philip said.

"The people who own the house, mugwump! If we wasn't there, they could sell it for thousands and thousands of pounds. I bet your Dad paid a fortune for this place."

"I don't know," Philip said.

"Well, I'm telling you." Darcy propped himself up on one elbow and looked down at Philip. "All these houses round here, they've got very pricey. So they try and get rid of all the poor people that rent them, and sell them to rich ones."

"You're not poor," Philip said. "You've got all sorts of things we haven't got. Like an electric dryer and a piano."

"Not a house, though. That's being poor, not having a house of your own," Darcy said. The colour rose in his face. "Or a dog," he said angrily.

Philip said, "My grandmother isn't allowed to have a dog, and she isn't poor. It's just one of the rules for people who live in the castle. And her apartment doesn't belong to her, she doesn't even pay rent for it. The Queen just lets her live there."

He wondered if the Queen would turn his grandmother out if she broke the rules and had a dog or a cat. Lady Anstruther had a canary, but perhaps that was different.

Darcy said, "I seen the Queen once. Last year, at the Jubilee. We all went and sat on the pavement and waved. Waste of time, really. Hours and hours waiting, and then she went by in about half a minute."

"I've never seen her at all," Philip said. "But I've got a Jubilee mug."

"Mine broke," Darcy said. "My Dad had a fancy to have his tea in it. He thinks a lot of the Queen. But he dropped it."

"You can have mine if you like."

"Don't be daft."

"It's not daft. I've got two of them, actually. One I got from school and one my grandmother gave me. I left that at home but I've got the school mug. I brought it to put my pens and things in . . ." Philip scrambled up, full of excitement, took the mug from the top of the book shelves and emptied the pens out. "Here," he said. "It looks a bit mucky but you can drink out of it if you wash it."

"Well." Darcy hesitated, frowning at Philip. At last he said, reluctantly, "All right, if you want to."

Philip gave him the mug. He said, "Thank you, Darcy."

"What are you thanking me for?"

"I don't know," Philip said. He couldn't explain how he felt, so happy and warm inside. He shook his head helplessly.

"Mugwump," Darcy said, "you really are an old mug-wump," and Philip grinned joyfully.

They were proper friends now, Philip thought. He had done something for Darcy; given him a present he wanted, and rescued the little cat. And, although it was never mentioned between them, he knew that Darcy still protected him from Adam and Moses. They teased him in class, flicking paper pellets when Miss Tomb's back was turned and putting lumps of chewed, squidgy gum on his chair, but they kept their distance outside in the playground, and when school was over Darcy was always there, waiting for him at the gate.

Darcy came to school every day now. Partly for Philip's sake, and partly because Addie was having a baby. "You have to be careful when women are pregnant," he explained to Philip. "Not to upset them, and that. And she'd be upset if she thought I was truanting."

"She doesn't look as if she were having a baby," Philip said. "She's not fat."

"Oh, it doesn't show yet. It's only just started."

"How does she know then?" Philip asked. Although he knew more than most boys about arthritis and bad backs and tunnel vision, he didn't know much about babies.

"The Doctor told her, of course," Darcy said. "She was feeling sick in the mornings and she went to see him. It won't be born till next winter."

Philip said, "But that's not for ages and *ages*."

The evenings were stretching out, longer and warmer. Spring became summer. They fished in the canal at the end of Philip's garden and roamed the more desolate reaches down-stream, below the lock, playing Philip's Famous Explorer game, stalking savage tribes through the weeds and the brambles that grew against the walls of the old, empty factories, and watching the broken windows for enemies. Gangs of thieves, Philip said, or robbers, or murderers, but Darcy said if anything lived in the tumble-down buildings it was more likely to be the ghost of Early Industrial Man.

This seemed a brilliant idea to Philip. He was proud that his friend was so clever. He knew he could never be as clever as Darcy, nor as strong, but he did his best to be like him in other ways. He refused to have his hair cut, copied Darcy's way of walking along hands in pockets and whistling, and tried to talk like him.

"I ain't got no decent letters," he said to his father when they were playing Scrabble one Sunday morning.

"Don't say ain't," his father said sharply.

"Darcy does."

"That's no reason why you should."

Philip looked at his father and saw his long nose had reddened. He said, "You like Darcy, don't you?"

"Yes, yes, of course," his father said. "He's a sensible boy." He gazed at the Scrabble board but his mind wasn't on it. He cleared his throat suddenly. "In fact, I've been wondering if his father would mind if Darcy spent a night here occasionally. Kept you company while Maggie and I were out for the evening."

"You can go out when you want to," Philip said. "I don't mind."

c*

"Maggie does, though. I know we have left you once or twice but she always worries. You're too old for a baby sitter, but she hates to think of you being alone."

Philip thought for a minute. Then he said, cunningly, "I could have a dog. If I had a dog, I wouldn't be alone, would I?"

His father laughed and shook his head. "Sorry, old love, but it's not very practical. You could ask your grandmother, but I don't think she's allowed to keep a dog in the castle, is she?"

"But I'm living here now," Philip said.

His father looked at him. He said, slowly, "I was thinking of when you go back in the summer holiday. Not long now, is it?"

"Maggie could look after the dog for me, couldn't she?" Philip slipped off his chair and said, eagerly, "Shall I go and ask her?"

"Not just now," his father said. "I think she's washing her hair. No point in it, anyway. I'm going to America to do a programme at the beginning of August, and she's coming with me."

"Can I have a dog when you come *back* from America, then? Next term?"

"Next term?" his father repeated. Philip wondered why he sounded surprised, but he was too excited to wonder for long.

"It starts in September," he said. "You'll be back by then, won't you?"

He felt very happy. If his father bought him a dog, he and Darcy could share it. Darcy would be so pleased when he told him.

His father said nothing. He was stroking his chin with his strong, bony fingers as if feeling for bristles, and watching Philip . . .

There was an odd look in his eyes, Philip thought. A bit shy. But that was silly, of course. His father could never be shy. Perhaps he just didn't like making promises.

Philip said, "You don't have to promise. Just think about it. After you've been to America. After the holidays."

"We'll see," his father said.

"I'm going to have a dog next term," Philip said to his grandmother when he spoke to her on the telephone as he always did, Sunday evenings.

"Next term?"

"Yes. I can't have one now because they're going to America and I couldn't bring it to the castle, could I? Has Lady Anstruther still got her canary?"

"Dead," his grandmother said. "I offered to buy her another one but she said, no thank you, she was too close to the grave herself to take on another young life. What's this about a dog?"

"I really want one for Darcy. He wants a dog more than anything, and he can't have one because the people they rent their house from don't allow it. And Darcy says, if they break the rules they'll be turned out, so they have to be careful."

"Darcy, Darcy!" his grandmother said. "That's all you talk about lately. How is his poor father's arthritis?"

"Much better lately since the weather's been warmer. He's been able to get out in the garden and he's even able to

75

do a bit of weeding. Bing made him a sort of low trolley and he shuffles along on it. Of course he still grumbles. I think he likes grumbling. Like Lady Anstruther."

"Don't be rude, Philip. Did you tell Mr Jones that a Posture Cushion might help him?"

"I told Addie, and she said that she'd see about it. Has your back been playing you up?"

"No more than usual. If old age is a sin, I'm not being punished too much," his grandmother said. "Though whether I'm spry enough to be much company for you in the holidays is another matter. I daresay you'll miss your friend Darcy."

"I suppose I will, really. But it can't be helped, can it? I mean, I've got to miss *someone*. I miss you when I'm here and I expect I'll miss him when I'm *there*." Philip sighed hugely.

His grandmother was quiet for a moment. Then she said, "What is Darcy going to do in the holidays?"

"Stay at home, I expect. I mean, they can't really go anywhere, not with Mr Jones being an invalid. Bing can get him into the van to go out for a day, but he likes his own bed at night. He likes things his own way altogether. He's a selfish old man."

He expected his grandmother to object to this but she didn't. She only said, "Being ill and in pain makes you selfish. Unless you're a saint."

"Addie is a saint," Philip said. "The way she looks after him. Bing and Darcy help, but she does the most of it."

"Could she manage for a while without Darcy, do you think?"

"I expect so. 'Specially now, in the summer, with Mr Jones being able to do a bit more for himself." Philip stopped. Then said, "*Oh!* Do you mean he could come and stay with us? Really? Oh, *Grandmother!*"

"Don't get excited," his grandmother said. She sounded as if she were smiling. "It may come to nothing, but there is no harm in asking. Only it must be done properly. Maggie must go and call on his father. Run along, Philip dear, and tell her I'd like a word with her."

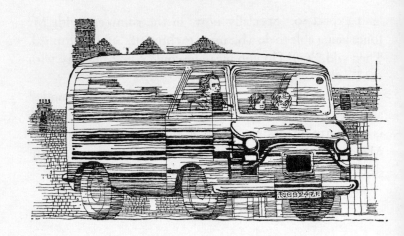

Chapter 6

It was too good to be true. Philip was so excited sometimes just thinking about it that he forgot to breathe, and only remembered to start again when his head started buzzing.

Although Darcy never said so, he was as excited as Philip. Now and again, when they were fishing, or just walking along the canal, he would suddenly turn red and whistle, a long, shrill, single note, and look shyly at Philip.

Only three more weeks of term. Only two. Only one . . .

Bing was to drive them down in his van. Darcy said there was a dealer he wanted to visit in Canterbury, but Philip guessed that Mr Jones had told him to take them.

"Only right we should do our bit," Mr Jones said, when Philip went to tea, the last day. "No trouble to Bing, and a help to your parents, young Philip. They'll be busy, I daresay, getting ready to go to America. A business trip, is it?"

"I don't know," Philip said.

"I should think so," Mr Jones said. "A man in your father's position. He must be as well known in the States as he is here, in England. I enjoyed his programme on Turkey the other night. Glad to see him back in harness again. Tell him that, will you? And tell your stepmother that we appreciated her coming here to invite Darcy to stay with you. A fine young woman, I thought, very gracious."

"My father would have come too," Philip said, feeling uncomfortable. "Only he had to see a man about something."

"Oh, I wouldn't expect it," said Mr Jones. "And your grandmother, Mrs Holbein Senior, wrote me a charming letter. I couldn't reply, I'm afraid, my fingers can't hold a pen, but I hope that you'll take a bunch of my roses and give them to her with my compliments."

"My grandmother is very fond of roses," Philip said. "Especially red ones."

"Sweets to the sweet," Mr Jones said. "Red roses it shall be."

They were sitting in the little back garden. High brick walls trapped the warm scents of summer; roses, sweet peas and pansies. Addie came out with a laden tea tray and Darcy jumped up to help her.

"That's too heavy, Addie," he scolded her. "You shouldn't be carrying trays as heavy as that."

Addie smiled. "I'm not an invalid, chicken."

"I know that. I only meant it might hurt the baby."

Addie patted her stomach. "He'll be all right. Tough as boots, the young ruffian."

"How do you know it'll be a boy, Addie?" Philip asked curiously.

Addie winked at him. "Mr Jones is expecting a boy." Her voice bubbled with laughter.

"My first grandson," Mr Jones said importantly. "It'll look well on the shop front. Bing Jones and Son. Antiques and Bygones. That's how I see it." He looked at Philip. "Your grandmother will have a lot of antiques, I expect."

"Well. She's got a lot of old furniture."

"Bound to be antiques in a castle," Mr Jones said. "Suits of armour, that sort of thing. History. Darcy is a lucky boy to have this grand opportunity. I hope he behaves himself." He looked sternly at Darcy who sighed and rolled his eyes upwards. "I expect Bing will be interested, anyway," Mr Jones said. "I hope he will have a chance to pay his respects to your grandmother, Philip. Though he won't have much time, of course. He has a lot on his plate tomorrow. He'll have to make an early start. I hope that won't be an inconvenience to your good parents."

"My father often has to get up early when he goes to the studios," Philip said.

"Four o'clock suit you, then? That's the time Bing was planning on, isn't it, Addie? So he can take in the silver market on the way."

Darcy nudged Philip. His green eyes were shining. "I fixed that with Bing! Told him you'd like it."

"Oh!" Philip said. "Thank you, Darcy."

He was so excited at the prospect in front of him that he

stopped breathing again until Darcy thumped him between the shoulder blades. He said, laughing, "Nothing much to see, mugwump, not really."

It wasn't so much what they saw as what they didn't see that made it exciting, Philip decided. Although the sky was streaked yellow with dawn, down in the narrow lanes of the city, between the high buildings, the night was still lingering. There were no market stalls, only estate cars and small vans parked along the sides of the lanes, their backs open, and men peering in, talking softly. Flickering torches, whispering voices, the clink of metal on metal and the occasional bright gleam of silver when a man lifted the sacking that covered it.

"It's like a treasure hunt," Philip said, when Bing hustled them back into the van. "Why is it so secret?"

"Just the way it is in this business," Bing said as he started the engine. "Not the best day, though. Prices are up, being good weather. Best time is when it's raining. Not so many buyers turn up and more chance of a bargain."

"Did you get anything?"

"Not for the stall. Just a private purchase." Bing fished something out of his pocket and gave it to Philip who was sitting on the bench seat between him and Darcy. It was a tiny mug; a silver mug for a baby.

"Georgian," Darcy said. "Very old. A real beauty. Christening mug for His Lordship."

"It's lovely," Philip said. "Do you want a boy, Bing? Mr Jones wants a boy, doesn't he?"

"Want may have to be his master," Bing said, and

chuckled. "I wouldn't say so to our Dad, of course, but I'd rather have a girl, personally. A tall girl, like my Addie."

"Whatever it is, it can't be quite like her, can it?" Darcy said. "I mean, it's bound to be paler, with you being the father."

"Coffee coloured, I expect. A mixture of both of us."

"If it was brown, with red hair and freckles, it would look awfully funny," Philip said.

"Nature don't make that sort of mistake somehow," Bing said. "Surprising, when you think, really."

"What are you going to call it?"

"Christian if it's a boy, Christine for a girl. That's what Addie has set her heart on."

"I'll be an uncle," Darcy said. He dug Philip in the ribs. "Uncle Darcy!"

This seemed wonderfully funny to Philip. He laughed at the idea of Darcy being an uncle, and because he felt happy.

Stopping at a red light, Bing looked down at him, grinning broadly. "Glad to be going home," he said. "Aren't you, sonny?"

They stopped on the way to have breakfast; eggs and bacon and tea. Philip was hungry but he couldn't eat; his stomach was churning. He was impatient, and, as they bowled down the motorway, he began to be frightened. When they drove through the ragged outskirts of the town to the sea and saw the castle on the green headland above it, he felt sick with fear. Suppose something had happened! Suppose she had died, last night, suddenly! Suppose she had forgotten that they were coming!

She opened the door. Philip flew into her arms. They closed round him tightly. She said, "Well, well, *well*!"

Philip gasped and trembled all over. His grandmother held him and looked into his face. She said, "What you want, Philip, is a glass of cold water."

His ears sang as he drank it. Through the singing, he could hear Bing and his grandmother talking. They were sitting down, a tray on the round, polished table between them. Coffee for Bing, lemonade and biscuits for Philip and Darcy. Everything ready. Slowly, Philip's ears came back to normal. His grandmother smiled at him. She said, "Take Darcy to your room, Philip. I've put a bed in there for him. You can unpack and put your clothes away while Mr Jones and I drink our coffee."

Philip led Darcy up the stairs to his round, turret room. "That's my grandfather's picture," he said. "That's my mother's."

Nothing had changed except for the extra bed his grandmother had made ready for Darcy. There was a low table beside it with a reading lamp and a little vase with a posy of violets.

Philip said, "Did you give her the roses?"

"She put them in water. While you was having a fit of the vapours." Darcy strolled round the room, hands in pockets. He went to the window and gave a low whistle. "You can see the sea, can't you?"

"Course you can, mugwump!" Philip's head started buzzing again. He sat down on his old bed and familiar springs twanged beneath him. He said, "I could die, I'm so happy."

At first, happiness felt like a blown egg in his hands; frail and easily broken. Often, in the first few days, he held his breath with fear as well as excitement. But little by little, this strange feeling left him. He was at home with his grandmother and it was as if he had never been away from her. Nothing had changed, except that Darcy was with them, doing all the things they had always done, looking for bottles with messages in them, picking up shells from the shore, and twisty shapes of pale driftwood, and getting up early, when the tide was right, to go shrimping. They swam from the shelving, pebbly beach, and took picnics up on the headlands, and came home in the evening for singing and games. Darcy always won at Scrabble and Philip always won at Monopoly and his grandmother always won when they played Racing Demon.

"You cheat, you know," Darcy told her. "That's why you always win."

"You're allowed to cheat a bit when you're old," Philip's grandmother said calmly.

"You're not very old, Mrs H," Darcy said. "I mean, you don't *act* old. Look at you this morning when we went shrimping! Knee deep in cold water!"

Philip's grandmother laughed like a girl. She said, "Flatterer! Let's hear you use that golden tongue to a better purpose," and sat down at the piano.

She made Darcy sing scales. She was stern with him when he sang, as she had never been stern with Philip. "You never made me sing scales," he said, feeling jealous.

"You can sing scales if you like," his grandmother said. "Any time. But Darcy's voice is something to take special care with. A gift from God. It's his duty to make the best use he can of it."

Philip was embarrassed because she had said this in front of Darcy. He thought Darcy would laugh, but instead he went red, then so white that the freckles on his cheeks stood out like small stones. He said, looking down at his feet, "Addie wants me to try for the cathedral choir school. That's a special boarding school for boys who sing in the choir."

"I'd hate to go to a boarding school," Philip said.

"I wouldn't mind if they taught you to sing," Darcy said. "Though I'd really rather sing in a theatre, I think. I mean, I sing in our church choir already."

"Then you must practise," Philip's grandmother said. "Not just when you feel like it, but when you don't, too. What we must do now is set you a target. Before the end of the holidays, we'll give Lady Anstruther a concert. She used to be a singer when she was young. Her husband heard her sing in a musical and went round to the stage door and met her. Only that was before he became an Air Marshal, of course."

"She doesn't like hymns," Philip said. "She's an artist. She told me that once, when I asked her why she didn't go to church."

"An atheist, I think she meant," his grandmother said. "Silly woman. Never mind, that's her business. Darcy will sing *Greensleeves* for her, and *Voi che sapete*."

"What's that?"

"Italian," his grandmother said. "An aria from *The Marriage of Figaro*. A song about love."

"Love!" Philip said scornfully. "Darcy can't sing about *love*. In *Italian*!"

"No such word as can't," his grandmother said automatically, but although she was smiling, it was a firm smile, and Philip knew there was no point in arguing.

Darcy practised the songs every morning while Philip made breakfast, and again in the evening, while Philip was having his bath, but he never sang them for Lady Anstruther.

They went swimming one afternoon. After three weeks of blue, blazing skies, the weather had turned cloudy and colder and when they came out of the sea they were goosey and shivering. Philip's grandmother rubbed them down with a rough towel and, when they were dressed, told them to run about and get warm while she went home to get their tea ready.

They ran on the beach, and skimmed stones, and climbed the slippery breakwaters and shouted; the wind took their voices and tossed them back like an echo. They came back to the castle, glowing and hungry and sticky with salt that made their hair stiff and tightened their faces, to find Addie waiting. She smiled once, to greet them when they came running in, but while they ate cinnamon toast and buttery scones and cherry cake, she sat in a chair by the window looking out at the sea, very straight-backed, very quiet, not smiling at all.

She had come to take Darcy home.

"Only a few days early. He was going at the end of the week anyway," Philip's grandmother said when they had gone and Philip burst out with questions.

"But why?" Philip asked. "Why *now*? She didn't say."

"You didn't ask her. Nor did Darcy, I noticed."

"She was so *quiet*," Philip said. "It made us feel funny. But she must have told you before we came in."

They were in the kitchen, washing the dishes. Philip looked at her angrily. "Tell me," he said. "Or I'll twist your arm. I'll give you a *Chinese burn*."

His grandmother washed the last cup slowly and carefully and put it down on the draining board. "Bing has been arrested by the police, Philip. He's in Brixton prison. Addie is allowed to visit him every day and she wants Darcy home, to stay with his father." She dried her hands and sighed. "That poor woman! Poor Darcy!"

Philip felt hot, then cold, and then hot again. He said, "It's not true. What's Bing done?"

"He's been charged with receiving. That means, buying and selling things other people have stolen. Until the case comes up in court, he's been remanded in custody. Kept in prison."

Philip breathed hard. "Did he do it?"

"I can't tell you that, can I?"

"He didn't," Philip said. "I know that he didn't. Bing isn't wicked."

"Wicked is a big word," his grandmother said. "It means more than just breaking the law. It means living wrongly."

"Breaking the law is wrong, isn't it?"

His grandmother didn't answer. She looked tired; her mouth was pursed up, the skin round it wrinkled and furry. She went out of the kitchen and into the living room. She sat by the window.

Philip followed her. He felt, suddenly, rather excited. He said, awed, "I've never known anyone who's gone to prison before. What's it like? Is it a dungeon?"

There were dungeons under the castle, with iron rings in the dark, dripping walls, and no windows. On Tuesdays and Thursdays, when the public parts of the castle were open, tourists came to look at these dungeons, peering through the small grilles in the heavy old doors.

"I think modern prisons are rather more civilised," Philip's grandmother said. "Though I don't suppose they are very comfortable."

"Do they feed you on dry bread and water?" Philip asked, thinking of prisoners in books who gave crumbs to mice and made friends with them.

"Not nowadays," his grandmother said. "And, if you are thinking of Bing, in this country you are innocent until you're found guilty. So I imagine that Addie is allowed to take him a good meal every day."

Philip said, "I love Addie."

"I can understand that," his grandmother said.

She was quiet for a little. Philip sat down on a stool at her feet and leaned against her for comfort, and wondered if Addie had told Darcy yet that Bing was in prison.

His grandmother said, "Philip, darling," and he looked up, astonished, because she hardly ever said *darling*.

She was looking out of the window at the grey sky, the grey sea. He saw her baggy throat move as she swallowed. She said, "Have you decided? Whether you want to stay here, or go back to London? We said we would talk about it this summer. Then you said you were getting a dog, and it seemed you had made your mind up. However your father might feel about it."

"Oh, he didn't *promise* to buy me a dog," Philip said. "He just said, we'll see, and I suppose that really meant no. So I won't ask again."

"That's not what I meant," his grandmother said. "I may be wrong, mind, but I had the idea that your father imagined you wouldn't want to go back to him after the holidays."

"Well, I suppose I don't," Philip said. "But I think he's expecting me."

As soon as he had spoken he realised that he wasn't sure about this. When they had talked about the dog, his father had sounded surprised. He had said, "Next term?" in that surprised voice . . .

Philip said, "Maggie is expecting me, anyway. She says, now my father is working again, I'm company for her."

"She's a nice girl," his grandmother said, rather absently. She stroked Philip's stiff, salty hair. "But you know, if she didn't have you to look after, she could travel a bit with your father."

"I think he'd like her to," Philip said. "He wanted to ask Mr Jones if Darcy could come and stay sometimes. We'd be all right, me and Darcy, if they wanted to go away for a weekend or something."

"You're both too young to be left alone," his grandmother said. "I'm surprised at your father. Though I suppose that I shouldn't be. I've known him a long time." She stopped and sighed. Then added, to herself, it seemed, "He makes use of people."

She spoke as if she didn't much like him, Philip thought, but of course that couldn't be true, since she was his mother. Perhaps she had meant that asking Darcy to stay, to keep Philip company, was "making use" of him. If Darcy felt that, he wouldn't like it. Darcy was proud.

Philip leaned against his grandmother's hard, bony knee and thought how proud Darcy was. Not boastful, just proud. That first time he had come to tea and talked to Philip's father about Mr Jones quoting Shakespeare, and Bing saving up for his shop, he hadn't been boasting, just showing that he was proud of his family, even though none of them were famous, like Henry Holbein.

And now Bing was in prison.

Philip said, "I want to stay here with you, of course I do, really. Only there's Darcy. If I stayed now, I'd be a traitor."

He looked up at his grandmother and saw she was smiling.

He said, "I mean, he's my *friend*."

His grandmother said, "Then there is no more to be said. I will speak to your father."

Chapter 7

Maggie said, "I was so sorry to hear about Darcy's brother. I wondered . . ."

"Wondered what?" Philip said.

"Whether I should go and see Addie. But your father thought . . ." She stopped and looked at Philip anxiously. "I'm sorry he isn't here. Your first evening."

"I don't mind," Philip said. "Why did he think you shouldn't go and see Addie?"

"He said it would be intruding. I just thought it was neighbourly. But I expect he knows best."

Philip thought she was looking unhappy. She wasn't

91

eating her supper. Perhaps she was missing his father, who had flown to Scotland that morning.

He tried to think of something to cheer her up. "Did you have a nice time in America, Maggie?"

"My brothers had grown. I hardly recognised them. Real skinnymalinks, as your grandmother would say."

Philip wondered if they looked like her. He said, without thinking, "Are they Red Indians, too?"

Maggie smiled at him. "Only a quarter. Our grandmother was Cherokee."

"I thought you might be a Red Indian," Philip said. "Darcy did, too. Only we didn't like to ask, really. It seemed a bit personal."

He was glad to hear Maggie laugh. She tossed her black braid back. "Well, you'll have something interesting to tell him tomorrow. Why don't you call for him and go to school with him?"

Philip looked at his plate. His heart thumped with shyness. "He usually calls for me."

Maggie said, "Then it would make a change, wouldn't it?"

"I ain't going to school," Darcy said. He wasn't looking at Philip. Although they had been walking side by side several minutes, he hadn't once looked at him.

They reached the canal bridge. Philip said, "Darcy, do you know something? Maggie really is a Red Indian. Her grandmother was a Cherokee. Why aren't you going to school?"

"Got something better to do." Darcy stood on the bridge and looked down at the canal. A few yellow leaves were floating on the dark surface. He said, watching the water, "Bing's coming up in the court today. He don't want Addie to go, with her being pregnant. And my Dad can't, of course."

Philip held his breath until he felt dizzy. He said, "Shall I come with you, Darcy? I don't care about school."

"Don't be daft," Darcy said. "It ain't none of your business. Besides, you'll get into trouble."

"My father's in Scotland," Philip said.

Darcy looked at him then, close and sad. He sighed deeply and shook his head. "They won't let you in, they don't let little kids in."

He set off at a fast pace and Philip followed him.

The court smelled of old clothes and cigarette smoke. It was crowded with people smoking and talking; tall policemen holding their caps under their arms, ushers in black robes, and women with wailing babies.

"They do let kids in," Philip said to Darcy indignantly.

"Not inside the courts, stupid. This is just the place where you wait for your name to be called. I think Bing's coming up in Court One, but I got to make sure. You wait here."

He disappeared in the crush. Philip stood by the wall. No one took any notice of him; he might have been a fly, or a beetle, he thought, as people shoved their way past, treading on his toes, squashing him. The smell made him feel sick. "What a stinky place," he said, when Darcy reappeared suddenly, ducking up between two men in dark raincoats.

"People sweat when they're scared," Darcy said. "It's a

known fact. Bing's in Court One, all right, I seen his lawyer. He says if we're sharp we can get in the gallery."

An usher stood by an open door, guarding it. He was very fat, very tall; Philip looked up the slope of his stomach, bulging out of his gown, and saw dark hairs sprouting from the caves of his nostrils. A woman spoke to him, touching his arm, and he turned to her and looked at a list in his hand. Darcy clutched Philip's sleeve and they slipped, unobserved, through the door. "Quick," Darcy breathed. "Go on to the end. He's not seen us."

Light filtered through high, dirty windows. There was more air in this big room, and no smoke, but the same old-clothes smell; musty and damp like a school cloakroom. Darcy and Philip slid along a narrow bench and a big man and several women came in behind them. The big man sat next to Darcy, hitching his trousers, spreading his knees, settling down comfortably. He grinned at the boys. He had two gold teeth in the front of his mouth and a blue scar on his cheek.

Philip thought—*Like a pirate*! He was scared for a minute; then the big man winked cheerfully and produced a packet of peppermints out of his pocket. "Go on lads," he said. "Be my guests. Take a couple."

They sat, sucking the peppermints. From the gallery, it was like looking down on a theatre. Tables and chairs and a dock in the centre, and a table on a raised platform facing it. Someone shouted, "Be upstanding in Court," and two men and a woman came through a door at the back of the platform and sat down behind the long table.

Everyone stood up and sat down. Philip wanted to go to

94

the lavatory but it was only fear; he squeezed his legs and shut his eyes tight until it passed off. When he opened them, a policeman was standing beside the platform and holding a Bible and saying, "I swear by Almighty God to tell the truth, the whole truth, and nothing but the truth." And there was a man in the dock.

Philip said, "That's not Bing," and Darcy jabbed him in the side with his elbow.

"Shut up," he whispered fiercely, "they always take the drunks and the tramps first," and Philip saw that the man in the dock was very old and shabby with a mane of thin, greasy hair straggling over his tattered coat collar.

The people on the platform muttered together. The woman sat in the middle, the two men either side of her. They were all quite old, with grey hair.

"Magistrates," the big man with the scar said, speaking quietly but clearly. "Bleeding magistrates." Someone in the gallery giggled. The woman glanced up and the giggling stopped. She waited a moment; then spoke to the man in the dock. She said, "We are going to fine you five pounds this time, Mr Montrose, for being drunk and disorderly. Can you pay this fine now?"

The old man didn't answer. The woman glanced at the policeman and raised her eyebrows. The policeman said, "He had two pounds in his pocket, Madame Chairman."

The woman nodded. She leaned forward and said, "Then you will pay a pound now, Mr Montrose, and a pound every week until the fine is paid off. We are being lenient but I must warn you that we may have to be more severe if you come up before us again. You have had a lot of help from the social services. If only you would try to help yourself, just a little."

Her voice was polite, but Philip felt himself shrivel inside. She had spoken to the poor old man as if he were a fool, or a baby.

He didn't move until the policeman came forward to help him out of the dock. As he turned, Philip saw his face for the first time; old and heavy with sad, drooping eyes that showed red rims underneath. He was looking bewildered as if he didn't understand what had happened.

Several men appeared in the dock after him, charged with being drunk, or drunk and disorderly. Some of them came in through a door at the side of the court, from the small entrance hall; others straight up into the dock, from some stairs underneath. "Them's the ones from the cells, the real violent blokes," the scarred man informed the gallery, but too low for the magistrates to hear. He took another peppermint out of his pocket and put it into his mouth. He belched and said, "Pardon," and leaned back and closed his eyes. "Wake me up when the show starts," he murmured to no one in particular.

Bing was next. Philip didn't notice him arrive in the court. He had been too busy looking along the gallery at the other people there and wondering if they were waiting for one of their family to come up before the judges, or if they were just there for amusement, as the man with the scar seemed to be. Then he heard Darcy give a little grunt, as if he had a sudden pain in his stomach, and saw Bing in the dock. Although he could not have heard the small sound Darcy had made, Bing looked round, up at the gallery. He gave a quick smile, widening his eyes in what seemed like comic dismay before he turned back again to listen to what the policeman was saying.

Darcy was gripping the rail of the gallery. He was staring at his brother who was very smartly dressed in a grey jacket and trousers. Bing looked very smart altogether, Philip thought, standing straight, arms stiff at his sides, like a soldier on parade, and not at all pale or ill; if anything, he was fatter than Philip remembered. Philip was ashamed to find he felt disappointed. Although it would have been terrible if Bing had been tortured or kept in a dungeon, it would have been more interesting if he had looked a bit pale, a bit frightened . . .

Instead, now the policeman had stopped talking, he was leaning forward over the edge of the dock and chatting to a young man in a dark suit; relaxed and easy as if they were both at a party.

"That's his lawyer," the scarred man said, leaning across behind Darcy and breathing peppermint breath into Philip's face. "Bright young chap he looks, don't he? Bit young, though. Tell you straight, I'd want someone with a few years behind him, if I was in trouble."

The lawyer turned away from the dock and went back to his table. He said, "My client is ready to plead now, Your Worships," and sat down and shuffled some papers.

Philip wondered why he had called the three judges *Your Worships*. As if they were Gods, sitting up there on their platform. Then he saw Bing straighten his back and lift his head high. As he did so, a tight roll of flesh appeared just above his coat collar. It seemed to grow pinker as the list of things he was supposed to have bought to sell on his stall was read out, until it looked, Philip thought, like a little pork sausage that would spurt juice if you stuck a fork in it. He was just about to nudge Darcy and share this joke with him when Bing spoke, very loudly and clearly.

"Guilty," he said, in this clear, loud voice. "I plead guilty."

Darcy grunted again. Philip looked at him and saw that he was doubled up as if he really did have a bad stomach pain. He said, "Do you feel sick?" Darcy shook his head. There were beads of sweat on his forehead.

Bing's lawyer was on his feet, talking. He held the lapels of his jacket and rocked backwards and forwards. Philip didn't understand all he said but he understood most of it. Bing's lawyer said that his client had pleaded guilty because although he had not actually *known* that any of the items he had bought had been stolen, he could not honestly say he was quite sure that none of them were. When you were buying antiques, it was not always possible to discover exactly where they had come from. It was, Bing's lawyer said, "a natural hazard of this particular trade." He hoped that the magistrates would take this into account while they were deciding the sentence. Also the fact that Mr Jones's wife was expecting her first child and that he had a young brother and a crippled father to care for as well.

The lawyer sat down and the magistrates on the platform put their heads close together. The man on the right looked quite kind, Philip thought. He was going bald, but a nice, shiny bald, like a baby. This man sat back in his chair and looked at Bing, frowning; then, suddenly, up at the gallery, straight at Darcy . . .

The woman magistrate said, "We have listened to what has been said on your behalf, Mr Jones, but you have been charged with serious offences and it is the duty of this court to take them seriously. You will go to prison for six months."

That was all. It was over. Bing vanished down the steps inside the dock and the kind, balding man looked up at Darcy with a sad expression as if he knew, seeing Darcy's red hair, that he must be Bing's brother, and felt sorry for him.

"I want to pee," Darcy said.

The scar-faced man stood up and let the boys wriggle past him. He said, "Bleeding shame."

Outside the door of the gallery, the fat usher was waiting. He grabbed Darcy's arm and shouted, "You'd no business in there, you know that! Slipping past me! I've half a mind to report you."

Darcy moaned, under his breath, and Philip said angrily, "It was his *brother* in there! How would you like it, if you were in trouble, and no one came to see what was happening, no one from your family."

The fat usher glared down at Philip. His face darkened and the hairs in his nostrils were twitching. He said, "Why, you cheeky little bugger!"

Philip was too full of rage to be frightened. He stamped his foot and said, "Let Darcy go, now this minute! Or I'll call a policeman!"

His own voice boomed in his ears like the sea. Then he heard laughter. He looked round and saw people watching. He said, "It's not *funny*."

99

A woman said, "No, it's not, lovey." A huge woman with thick, bandaged legs, sitting on a chair by the wall. When she stood up, she was almost as tall as the usher. She said, "You heard, my friend. Leave the kid be."

The usher looked at her. She looked back at him levelly. She had a big, pale, sweaty face, surrounded by a frizz of orange-coloured hair. The usher let Darcy go and turned away, looking scornful. The woman winked at Philip and went heavily back to her chair.

Darcy stood, blinking. Bing's lawyer appeared and put his arm round his shoulders. He said, "Come along now. Both of you."

He led them into a little room off the hall and shut the door. There was no furniture; just bare boards and bare walls. Darcy started to cry and the lawyer gave him a handkerchief. Darcy blew his nose and handed it back. He said, "I've got my own handkerchief, don't know why I took yours."

The lawyer looked at him helplessly. He said, "I'm sorry. Please tell Mrs Jones that I'm sorry. But really, you know, it was the best we could hope for. If your brother had pleaded not guilty, they would have sent him to a higher court to be tried with a judge and a jury, and he might have been given a much longer sentence. As it is, with remission, he'll be out in four months. That's not too bad." He smiled encouragingly. "All things considered."

Philip was shocked by his smile. He said, severely, "It's bad for *Bing*, isn't it? And it isn't fair, either. I mean, back in there, you said that he didn't know those things were stolen. So you shouldn't have let them send him to prison."

"I'm afraid it isn't as simple as that," the young lawyer said. "I'm afraid . . ."

"Never mind what you're afraid of," Darcy said roughly. "I want to see Bing. Before they take him away. It's allowed, isn't it?"

"They wouldn't let you down in the cells. It's not suitable. You're not old enough. You shouldn't have been in court either. You know that, don't you?"

Darcy didn't answer. He was clenching his fists and his mouth was clenched too; tight and shivering. The lawyer looked at him and sighed. He put his hand in his pocket. "Here," he said, holding out a pound note, "get yourself something on the way home. An ice, or a coke."

Darcy couldn't speak. Philip spoke for him. "No thank you," he said. "It's very kind of you but we're neither of us very hungry just at the moment."

They sat beside the canal. Dead leaves drifted by on the slow water like fallen gold pennies. At last Darcy said, "I'd best get home, hadn't I? Tell Addie and Dad. They'll be waiting."

He winced as he got up like an old man with rheumatism. Philip wished he could do something to help him. Say something. All he could think of was, "It wasn't fair, Darcy."

"What's fair ain't got nothing to do with it," Darcy said. "You get on the wrong side of the law and you've had it. I reckon that's what Bing must have thought, anyway. I reckon he thought it was best to get it over and done with." He looked at Philip, biting his lip. "Thanks for coming."

"That's all right," Philip almost said that it had been the

most exciting morning of his whole life, but stopped himself in time. He blushed. "Tell Addie I'm sorry."

Darcy nodded. "You'd best get to school, hadn't you? Don't say where you've been, though." He hesitated, then mumbled, shame-faced, "Don't gab about it. Don't gab to *anyone*."

"Cut my throat and hope to die," Philip said, and realised, as he made this solemn promise, that it would be hard to keep.

He would have to lie. He would have to lie to Maggie and to his father. Even Maggie would be angry if she knew where he had been this morning, and his father—well, his father would be so furious that it made Philip queasy inside just to think of it.

He walked slowly to school. It was just after one o'clock. Dinner hour was over and everyone was filing in from the playground. Miss Tombs was at the top of the steps, the bell in her hand. She flashed her stone teeth and said, "Hallo Philip. Had a good holiday?"

"Yes, thank you, Miss Tombs."

He tried to slip past but she rolled her wild eyes at him. "You're in Mr Parson's class this term, aren't you?"

Philip felt hot and cold. Not only was he going to lie to his father and Maggie, but he was going to start lying now. He rubbed his clammy hands down the side of his jeans and remembered what Darcy had said. *People sweat when they're scared.* He was scared of lying because lying was wicked. But Miss Tombs was waiting. He said, "I don't know, Miss Tombs. I've only just come to school. I've been ever so sick all the morning."

Chapter 8

Philip was not punished for the lies. Miss Tombs believed him, and Maggie. Perhaps they were what his grandmother meant by white lies, Philip thought; things that you had to say, to stop worse things from happening.

He said to Maggie that evening, "Bing got sent to prison today. Darcy told me. He didn't come to school but I met him on the bridge on the way home and he told me. But he doesn't want people to know. So you mustn't tell anyone."

"Oh," Maggie said. Her eyes were dark and sad. "Oh, Philly, how dreadful!"

"Darcy was crying," Philip said. At least *that* wasn't a lie—

or not altogether. Darcy had cried at the court. He said,
"What'll happen to them all, Maggie? If Bing is in prison
they won't have any money to live on. They'll *starve* . . ."

Maggie said gently, "They won't starve, Philly love.
I expect Mr Jones has a pension. And they'll get Welfare
money. What you call in England, Social Security. Besides,
Addie works, doesn't she? Though I suppose she'll have
to stop soon because of the baby. I wish there was something
we could do, Philly."

"Perhaps my father can," Philip said. He thought of his
father, talking on television about all the wrong things that
went on in the world and a good idea came to him. "I mean,
since he's famous. If he said it was wrong that Bing got
sent to prison, went on the telly and said it, he might get
him set free."

Maggie was sucking the end of her braid like a little
girl. "I shouldn't say anything to him if I were you, honey."

"But he knows about Bing, doesn't he? Didn't grandmother tell him?"

"Yes, she did. But I don't think he'd want to discuss it
with you. It might worry him."

"Why should it worry him? I mean, *he's* not shut up
in prison."

"I think he might be upset, knowing that you knew all
about it." Maggie smiled at him nervously. "You shouldn't
be mixed up in this sort of thing, Philly. With people
in this sort of trouble. That's what would worry him.
You're only a little boy and he is responsible for you.
After all, he's your father."

Philip said, amazed, "But Darcy's my *friend*."

★　★　★

The next day, after school, he went home with Darcy. He was shy at first, expecting some dreadful change, but although Addie was quieter than usual, she played the piano for them, and when Darcy had sung the two songs Philip's grandmother had taught him, she fetched a cake from the kitchen and cut big slices for both of them.

Until then, Mr Jones had not said a word. He hadn't sung with them, not even the easy hymns, just sat hunched in a chair by the fire in the little front room, looking like an elderly goblin. Then, as he munched his cake, his eyes darted slyly at Philip. He said, "I must say I'm surprised to see you here, Philip Holbein. Surprised that your father allows it!"

Philip looked at his plate. Addie said, "Now, Dad!" softly and warningly, but Mr Jones took no notice of her.

"Evil communications corrupt good manners," he said. "That is what I would think in Henry Holbein's position. We are no longer a respectable family. In disgrace with fortune and men's eyes."

His crippled hand shook and he spilled his tea. Addie got up from the piano stool, removed the wet rug from his knees, and re-filled his cup. She said, "Don't upset yourself with this kind of talk. It embarrasses Philip. And it doesn't help anyone."

"Allow me to be the judge of that, Addie," Mr Jones said. "I would like another spoonful of sugar in my tea, if you please, and permission to speak as I wish in my own house."

Darcy groaned. Mr Jones looked at him sharply, then said,

D*   105

to Philip, "The times are out of joint here, young man. We are outcasts from society. Pariahs. Addie puts a good face on it but she'll learn soon enough."

Philip concentrated on finishing his chocolate cake. It was delicious; a layer of soft cream in the middle and scrunchy icing with chopped hazel nuts in it.

"Our neighbours have been very good," Addie said. "I have had nothing but kindness. This cake comes from Mrs Willis next door. Would you like another slice, Philip?" She smiled at him. "Your grandmother has been so kind, chicken. I telephoned her yesterday, it seemed only right after her goodness to Darcy, and I had a letter by the first post this morning. She says she is praying that the Lord will help us to bear all our troubles. That was a great comfort to me."

"She'll have to pray pretty hard to get Dad to shut up," Darcy said.

"That's enough, Darcy," Addie said sternly. "It is not a matter to joke about. Your father is suffering."

Mr Jones ignored this exchange. "Mrs Holbein Senior is a very old lady. Very gracious and pious, but other people may not be so charitable, Addie. It is my duty to warn you of that. Wait till it gets about, girl! Then you'll see the skirts drawn aside, you'll see the cold shoulder! It'll be in the local paper at the end of the week, bound to be!"

"Oh, no one reads that old rag," Addie said.

Someone did. Friday afternoon, Philip found Darcy with his back against the wall in the playground, a ring of boys round him.

Philip pushed through them to Darcy's side. Darcy was saying, "I didn't know you could read, Moses Green!"

"Don't have to read very much, do I? That's your brother Bing, ain't it?" Moses held up a newspaper and jabbed at the page with his finger. Philip saw a picture of Bing and a headline. ANTIQUE DEALER JAILED.

Moses laughed. "Antique dealer! Rag and bone merchant, more like!"

Several boys tittered. Darcy said nothing. He looked glum and miserable.

Philip felt tight with anger. Something tinkled by his right foot. He bent down and picked up a lump of glass; the broken top of a bottle. He held it out like a sword, the jagged edge pointing at Moses, and said, "Shut up. You say one more word, Moses, and I'll cut your face open."

Just saying this made him feel shaky. He shut his eyes to steady himself but in his mind he saw the Joker's face slashed, the blood streaming. He drew a long breath, opened his eyes, and said, loud and clear, "So help me God, I'll cut you to red and white ribbons."

Moses was staring at him, his mouth hanging open. Then, to Philip's astonishment, he shrugged his shoulders and turned his back on them.

Darcy said, "You looked awful. Like a fiend. Honestly! You'd gone sort of *green*. I don't know if you scared Moses, but you sure as hell frightened me!"

"Don't go on about it," Philip said. "If I looked green, it was because I felt sick. I hate blood. Even just thinking about it."

They were feeding the ducks in the canal basin below the lock. Philip threw the last piece of the bread he had saved from school dinner. He said, watching a greedy gull swoop down and chase all the ducks away, "I hate bullies. I hate Moses Green."

"I hate Mrs Trumpeter more," Darcy said. "Moses is just an old talk box, *talking* don't hurt, but Mrs Trumpeter sacked Addie yesterday. Addie told her what happened to Bing, she had to tell her before she saw for herself in the paper, and the old hag gave her a week's wages and said she needn't bother coming again. As if she couldn't trust Addie not to pinch something!"

"Mean," Philip said. "Oh, that is *mean*. People like that ought to be shot! Oh, poor Addie, how horrible. How . . ."

"Don't go on," Darcy said. "Or I'll be sorry I told you."

They walked along the tow path in silence. There was a narrow boat in the lock. They watched it slowly rise up in the water.

Philip said, "You won't starve, will you, Darcy? Maggie says you can get Social Security."

Darcy shook his head. "Not while you've got savings. And we've got the money Bing was putting by for the rent of the shop. But Addie won't touch it. She says Bing has got to have something behind him when he comes home. She says she can get another job, easy. Though Dad says she shouldn't. He says she should rest up a bit with the baby. I wish I could get a job. I tried for a newspaper round but the man said I wasn't old enough. You've got to be thirteen, he said. It's the law. I said I was nearly thirteen, and he laughed."

"I've got money in my Post Office savings," Philip said.

Darcy looked at him. Just one look was enough.

"I'm sorry," Philip said sadly.

During the next few weeks, Philip thought a lot about money. Once, walking along the shore with his grandmother, he had found nearly two pounds in small coins, scattered along the edge of the sea as if they had fallen from someone's pocket. They had taken the money to the police station and Philip had signed his name in a book and after a while he had got the coins back because no one had claimed them.

He said, to Darcy, "If people lose money, as long as it's not very much, they don't bother going to the police station to see if anyone's found it. So we could look on the tow path, and if we found some, just a bit, it might be all right to keep it."

"*Just a bit* isn't enough," Darcy said.

Philip sighed. "In Italy, they throw coins into fountains for luck. My father told me. Perhaps foreign tourists throw coins in the fountains in Trafalgar Square. We could go and see, couldn't we?"

"Cost the bus fare to get there," Darcy said. "And they'd be foreign coins, anyway. Honest, Philip, there's nothing kids can do, really."

"Bills, bills, bills," Philip's father said, sorting his letters at breakfast. "Lord above! Electricity up, and the telephone!"

"How much is the electricity bill?" Philip asked.

"Eighty-two pounds. Why? Are you offering to make a contribution?"

"I just wanted to know," Philip said. "It seems very expensive."

"Living is expensive," his father said. "God knows how poor people manage."

"What would happen if you were a poor person and couldn't pay for the electricity?"

"You'd get cut off," Philip's father said. "The Electricity Company would cut off the supply." He yawned and pushed the bills across the table to Maggie. He said, "See to them, Maggie love, will you?"

Philip was glad to see that Mr Jones still had his electric fire burning in his basement room. It was important to keep warm with arthritis. But the television had gone.

Mr Jones said, "Lot of rubbish on nowadays, Philip Holbein. Not your father's programmes, of course, but the rest of it is just a diet for morons. Not worth the rent or the licence fee. I've decided to concentrate on my reading this winter. Brush up on Shakespeare. And on the Bible. Not that I'm religious mind, not like Addie, but there's a lot of inspiration there, in the old Bible. Tidings of comfort and joy."

"That's a carol," Philip said. "A Christmas carol."

"Go and sing it," Mr Jones said. "I feel like a bit of entertainment. Leave the door open and I'll hear from my bed."

"Early for carols, Dad," Darcy said. "Not yet November."

"Might as well look ahead," Mr Jones said.

Addie played the piano for them. She had another job, checking out in the supermarket. "Just for this month," she said. "I'll soon be too large to get behind the till." She patted her stomach and smiled.

"When will the baby come?" Philip asked.

"Due at the beginning of January. Might even be late December. A Christmas present for Bing." Addie looked sad for a moment, then lifted her head and said, "What about *Away In A Manger?*"

They sang, *"Away in a manger, No crib for a bed,"* and Philip thought about Addie's baby, growing big in her stomach, and wondered if she had got a cradle for him. While they were singing, he thought of a good way to make money to buy one.

"We could go singing carols," he said to Darcy when Addie had gone to the kitchen. "We could collect money and give it to Addie to buy things for the baby."

Darcy scowled. "People won't give you anything for yourself. Only for charity."

It would be a kind of charity, Philip thought. In church, they prayed for people in prison, so it would be all right to collect for Bing's baby. But he didn't say this to Darcy in case it offended him. He said, "There's no law to say you can't keep the money. And if you sing nicely, you've earned it." He looked at Darcy's doubtful face and added, slyly, "Besides, you like singing, don't you?"

"It's too early to go singing carols."

"Well, we've got to practise first, haven't we?" Philip said.

They practised most days, going to Darcy's house after school and getting tea ready for Addie. She was always willing to play the piano after a cup of tea. Although she looked tired when she came home from work, the carols seemed to revive her, and towards the end of the practice time she often sang along with them in a rich, strong voice that was surprisingly deep for a woman.

The days shortened. By mid-November it was almost dark when they came out of school and there was a dry, frosty nip in the air.

Philip said, "It's getting Christmassy. I can smell it. The hairs in my nose are going stiff."

"That's just cold," Darcy said. "Just winter. Not Christmas."

But the shops in the High Street were already decorated with holly and sparkling with tinsel. Darcy and Philip looked in a window at an electric train whisking busily in and out of tunnels and past toy railway stations. In a corner of this window there was a life-size Santa Claus with flashing red lights for eyes.

Philip said, "Oh, Darcy! We can start now, can't we?"

"I don't mind," Darcy said. "If you want to."

They only got one pound and forty pence the first week. Darcy was too shy to sing properly. He pulled faces from shyness and made Philip giggle and most of the time they ran away before anyone came to the door.

The next week was better. They started in a quiet back street outside a terrace house where there was a light in the downstairs front window. They sang, *O Come, All Ye*

Faithful, and when they had finished they heard footsteps in the hall. Someone called out, "Don't open the door, Mabel!" A gruff voice. They looked at each other and Darcy pulled one of his faces. Then the door opened, just a crack, on a chain, and they saw a tiny, whiskery face and a small, shaky hand, poking through. In spite of the whiskers, it was a little old woman, the same height as Philip. She whispered, "Quick, here you are, it was lovely, but go away, please. Mother gets angry . . ."

The gruff voice called, "Mabel, what are you up to?" and the little woman said, "Nothing, Mother, I'm coming," and closed the door gently.

She had given Philip a pound. He said, "Oh, Darcy, look . . ."

Darcy was frowning. "That's too much for one carol."

"We can't sing another," Philip said. "And we can't give the pound back. She'd get into trouble."

No one else gave them as much as that, but in the next four days they made six pounds altogether. They discovered that it was no use singing outside houses where they could see the television was on, and that they did better in the small, shabby streets than in the smarter terraces and squares where the houses were freshly painted and they could see new, shining kitchens through the lit, basement windows.

"That's how rich people get rich," Darcy said. "Keeping tight hold of their money."

"They can't all be stingy," Philip objected. "My father's quite rich, at least I think so, and I don't think he's mean. Some people came last Sunday morning for Cancer Research and he gave them five pounds."

"Cancer's different," Darcy said. "Are we going to sing at your house?"

"I don't know," Philip said. Maggie knew he was out singing carols but he wasn't sure if she realised that they were singing for money. She had said, "Have fun, honey," as if it were just a game he and Darcy were playing.

"Perhaps we better not," Darcy said, watching him.

Philip sighed. "Course we will," he said boldly.

The next Monday they started to work their way up Philip's street. They collected three fifty pence pieces, one ten penny piece, and a bar of chocolate. The house next to Philip's had a light in the second floor window. "That's where the old lady lives," Philip said. "The one with the cat that we rescued."

"The deaf lady? There's no point in singing to her if she's deaf."

"We don't know that she's deaf," Philip said. "It was just that you thought she might be."

They sang *The First Noël* and *Hark the Herald Angels Sing*, before the front door was opened. A stout man stood there, a short, roly poly man with a round stomach and a round, merry face. He wore a green velvet jacket and black velvet trousers and peered at them through thick glasses.

Philip said politely, "We're singing for Christmas," and the man beamed at them and said, speaking hesitantly, sounding foreign, "A most charming custom, my dears. I have been listening to you with pleasure and now I am come to invite you. It would please my Aunt Helga greatly if you would come in to sing to her. She is a little deaf and could not hear you as clearly as I could."

Darcy winked at Philip as they followed the man up the stairs. It was a warm, hushed, comfortable house; thick carpets under their feet and fine rugs hanging on the walls of the stair well, gleaming silkily in the soft, shaded light. In the drawing room on the first floor, the old lady sat in a high backed chair with the cat on her lap. Rings flashed on her fingers as she stroked the cat's head with one hand and smoked a long, thin cigar with the other. She was wearing a long black dress embroidered with crimson roses; above its high collar her face was pale and severe, her eyes hard and shiny as jet. She looked at Darcy and Philip and said something in a foreign language.

The roly poly man smiled at the boys. "My Aunt Helga greets you. It is her wish that you sing for her now."

He spoke as if this were a royal command and sat down. Sitting, with his round belly thrust forward, he reminded Philip of Humpty Dumpty. He choked back a giggle.

They sang, *Away in a Manger*, and *Once in Royal David's City*, and the old lady smoked her cigar and listened, watching them with her bright, beady eyes. When they had finished the second carol, she turned to her nephew and said in English, in a deep, gutteral voice, "The bigger boy sings like an angel. Ask him to sing alone, Heinrich."

Philip wondered why she didn't ask Darcy herself. Perhaps she thought she was too grand to address them directly. A proud, rich, rude old lady.

She was certainly rich. While Darcy sang, *As with gladness men of old, Did the guiding star behold*, Philip looked at paintings and velvet hangings and spindly legged chairs with tapestry seats and glass-fronted cabinets full of delicate ornaments and small, pretty pieces of polished silver. There was a gold clock under a glass dome on the mantelpiece and above the clock, a huge mirror in a gold frame reflected the rich, cluttered room and the old woman crouched in the middle of it. She looked like a spider, Philip thought suddenly; a glittering spider, guarding her treasure.

He had never seen so many beautiful things in one place before. It amazed him. He looked at Darcy and saw he was amazed, too. "*Holy Jesus, every day, Keep us in the narrow way,*" Darcy sang, and his green eyes danced round, bright and sharp, missing nothing.

Philip had never heard him sing so well. When he stopped, the room was still for a minute, as if the sweet voice had laid a spell on it. Then the old lady smiled briefly, showing yellow teeth, and lit another cigar.

Humpty Dumpty stood up. "Thank you, my dear children, that was very delightful. Now, to reward you, I will show you some of my Aunt's pretty things." He went to one of the cabinets and unlocked the door. "See," he said, picking up a silver box, "is this not quaint?" He snapped open the lid and inside the box there was a doll the size of a finger nail, tiny legs and arms quivering. "A child's toy," the man said. "Very old, very precious." He put the box back and showed them a little green lion with red stones on its head. "Jade," he said, "set with rubies. And this is even more valuable. This ivory ball, with many other small balls inside. A Maharajah gave it to my Aunt Helga, in India. A blind man has carved it. He was quite

116

young when he began and old when he finished. I often think of the years of his life that he spent, carving this for our pleasure . . ."

The old woman spoke sharply in her foreign language, and her nephew closed the cabinet door. He said, "That is all, I'm afraid. My Aunt is tired now."

He ushered them out of the room, down the stairs. When he had opened the door, he felt in the pocket of his velvet jacket, inspected the coins he took out, and gave Darcy one of them. Darcy looked at it. He said nothing, even when Philip cleared his throat to remind him, so Philip thanked the man for him. He said, "Thank you, Sir. Thank you for the money and for showing us all those nice ornaments. It was very interesting."

"My pleasure, dear child," the man said, and closed the door on them.

Darcy stood still on the pavement. He said, in a slow, angry voice, "Ten pence! That's all he gave me! And he had a fifty pence piece in his hand! I wouldn't have minded so much if *she* had said thank you *herself*!"

"Perhaps she felt shy, speaking English," Philip said. "I mean, I feel shy, speaking French. I suppose ten pence is a bit mean when we'd sung all those carols. But the man was nice, wasn't he?"

"Made me *sick*," Darcy said savagely. "Turned me up when he went on about that ivory ball."

He threw the coin in the gutter. Philip bent to retrieve it but Darcy grabbed his jacket to stop him. "Leave it," he said. "Leave it lie! I don't want it. I'm not singing for pennies no more!"

"Don't be daft, Darcy," Philip said. "We've got nearly nine pounds!"

"What's the good of that?" Darcy said. "It's no use . . ."

His voice was angry and grieving. "*Nothing's* no use," he mourned. "We could work all our lives like that poor old blind man in India. Nine pounds is nothing. You need hundreds and hundreds, just to pay bills! To buy groceries! D'you know what I thought when he showed us them things in that cabinet? Just *one* of them, I was thinking, *she* wouldn't miss it, and Addie wouldn't have to worry no more . . ."

He looked at Philip, his face stone-white and cold in the light of the street lamp and Philip felt his heart turn over with terror.

Chapter 9

"Sure they don't use that top room?" Darcy said. "You never seen *no one*? Not a light? *Nothing*?"

Philip shook his head. "Only the little cat, that one time. Someone must have been there, or it wouldn't have got shut in, would it?"

"I expect the old ~~bitch~~ has someone to clean. But that

would be mornings. Does anyone sleep there? *Visitors?* That fat man must be staying there."

"There wasn't a bed. Just the furniture, chests of drawers and a table. And the chair that I stood on."

Philip's mouth was dry. He tried to suck spit from the sides of his mouth to moisten his tongue and wished Darcy would stop. But he was frightened to say so. He was frightened of Darcy. He had never seen him like this before. All the time they had been having tea with Maggie he had not said a word except "Please" and "Thank you". Just sat at the table like a cold, angry stranger.

Even now they were alone in the attic he didn't seem like the Darcy he knew, Philip thought. He had changed. He was different. Something about his stern face, set and pale under his flaming hair, reminded Philip of his grandfather's photograph in his room at the castle. But that was silly. Darcy was only a boy. He wasn't a soldier.

Darcy said, "I sang my best for her and she didn't even say thank you. The old hag, the old *toad.*"

He spoke quietly in a flat, remote voice that was somehow more sinister than if he had shouted. "You don't have to help me." His cold, green, stranger's eyes looked at Philip. "But I can't get in if you don't."

A general, Philip thought. *A general, sending his troops into battle!*

He felt his scalp prickle and creep. As if the top of his head was lifting off.

He said, "Even if—even if we got something, what would we do with it?"

"Sell it up the market," Darcy said promptly. "One

of Bing's friends would take it off me and no questions asked. That part's easy."

Philip said, "All those things are locked up. When he showed us, he unlocked the cabinet. And he's *there*, anyway. And the old lady."

"They won't hear, two floors down," Darcy said. "And there'll be something in that top room. Bound to be. You leave that to me. All you got to do is let me in through the big window."

Philip wished he could have a heart attack suddenly. Or a stroke, like Lady Anstruther's husband. He had been paralysed for two months before he died, only able to move his eyes, she had told Philip's grandmother. If he was paralysed, Philip thought, he couldn't do anything. "I feel ill," he said faintly.

"Scared, that's all," Darcy said. Not sneering, just making a statement.

"Course I'm scared," Philip said. "Being scared has got nothing to do with it."

"You won't go to Hell, you know," Darcy said. "It's not like stealing from a poor person."

He smiled. Smiling, he looked like himself again, Philip thought. His friend, Darcy.

"I'd rather go to Hell than be a traitor," Philip said proudly.

They were out on the parapet. The wind lifted their hair and sang round the roofs and the chimney pots; it blew raggy clouds over the moon and made the bare trees creak and groan along the canal bank. Lights from the street lamps and houses trembled in the black water below them. The attic next door was dark. The little window was open.

"You've grown a bit since the last time," Darcy said. "You may be too big to get through."

"I can try," Philip said.

They stood close together, for warmth and for comfort. Philip could feel Darcy breathing; deep shudders inside his chest.

Darcy said, "You don't have to do it, you know. I mean, I'm not twisting your arm."

"I know." Philip's teeth chattered. "I'm just a bit cold," he said.

Darcy looked down at him. His eyes were deep pools; fathomless. "It was you started it, really," he grumbled. "Going on and on about money."

Five floors down, the kitchen door opened and Maggie stepped out into the garden. There was a splashing sound.

"What's she doing?" Darcy whispered.

"Emptying the tea pot round the camelia. Old tea leaves are good for plants."

"Suppose she comes up to your room and finds we're not there?"

"She won't," Philip said. "She never does, does she?"

"Always a first time," Darcy said grimly. "Suppose someone wants you? Your grandmother on the telephone."

"She only rings on Sunday. It doesn't cost so much, Sundays."

"It might be something urgent. She might have got ill or something."

"If she was ill, she wouldn't be able to telephone. Stop fussing, Darcy."

Thinking about his grandmother made Philip uneasy. In fact, now he had made up his mind, it was best not to think about anything. "All this old *talk*," he said, almost angrily. "Let's just get on with it."

Scrambling up the sloping roof, he was suddenly more exultant than frightened. After all, he had done this before and nothing had happened, no one had caught him. At the back of his mind he knew that he hoped they would find nothing worth stealing in the old lady's attic, but at least he would have shown Darcy that he was a real friend, a true friend. Not a traitor . . .

He slipped through the little window as he had done before—if he had grown, it was only taller, not broader— and stood for a moment to get his breath back. It was darker inside the room than outside, but enough light came through the window, from the moonlit, gusty sky, to see fairly clearly. The same dark, heavy furniture, the same coloured rugs on the floor. The only thing that was different from last time was a chess board on a small table with pieces set out as if someone had started a game and abandoned it. The chess men were pretty; Philip picked up an ivory Castle, a little round tower with a man's head poking out of the top, a soldier blowing a trumpet, and stroked it with his fingers, feeling the delicate carving.

Darcy rattled the window. He was pulling faces at Philip to tell him to hurry.

Philip put the Castle in his pocket and went to the window. It wasn't a sash window like the one in his attic, but two glass doors with brass handles, bolted into the sill at the bottom. He tried to lift one of the bolts but he couldn't move it; he felt under the knob at the top and found a small hole with the tip of his finger. He thought— *a round key*—and then saw it, hanging in the same place that his grandmother put the keys for her windows, on a nail on the wall at the side. He took the key off the nail and fitted it into the lock. It turned easily. He lifted the first bolt, then unlocked the second, and pushed the doors open.

And was, at once, deafened and blinded. A bell rang, jangling like a city fire engine, and a light, switched on at the same time as the alarm, a bright spot light, somewhere on the parapet, blazed in his eyes like white fire.

He stood, stunned and frozen. He heard Darcy shout, "Come on, you fool, *run* . . ."

Philip fell head first over the door sill, sliding along the gutter. He lay, moaning, dead leaves and slime under his cheek. Darcy dragged him up, rough hands under his arm pits, almost carrying him over the low wall between the two balconies. Philip's legs folded beneath him like rubber. "I can't . . ." he gasped. "I can't *stand*. You go, and leave me . . ."

"Don't be daft," Darcy said, and heaved him in through the window.

They collapsed on the floor of Philip's room as they had done after they had rescued the cat, but this time they were not laughing.

When he had got his breath back, Darcy got to his feet and closed Philip's window. He drew the curtains across it. Outside, the jangling alarm went on ringing.

Philip put his hands over his ears. Darcy crouched beside him and pulled them away. "You're covered in mud," he hissed. "And you're bleeding." He tried to wipe Philip's face with his handkerchief.

"I can do it," Philip said. He stood up, on his rubbery legs, and went to the wash basin. He looked in the mirror and saw his face staring out at him, ghost-pale under the streaked blood and dirt. He cleaned this ghostly face slowly. He felt slow and heavy as if he were moving about under water. He looked at Darcy and said, "Is that better?"

"A bit," Darcy said. "Try and act normal."

They sat on the bed. After what seemed several hours the alarm bell stopped ringing. The silence was worse, somehow. Then, breaking into the terrible silence, a sudden gust of wind howling and a shattering crash.

Darcy said, in a light, strained voice, "I think that was one of them doors. We ought to have shut them."

"Perhaps they'll think they just blew open in the wind and set the alarm off," Philip said hopefully. "If we want to act normal, then we ought to get out on the balcony and pretend we've come to see what has happened. Or go and call Maggie."

"No way," Darcy said. He didn't look like a general now. His shoulders were hunched, his face shrunken and wintry. Philip looked at him and thought—*when he gets old, he'll look like his father*!

Philip said, "You can go home if you want to. I mean, you would have gone home about now, wouldn't you? It's gone seven. So Maggie wouldn't think it was funny."

"I can't go leaving you," Darcy said.

"I don't mind."

"Well, I do. So shut up about it. Shut up, anyway. *Listen*!"

There was a *bang* from next door, and a tinkle, as if someone was closing the broken window. But the wind was blowing hard now, thumping against the walls of the houses like a heavy fist, and they couldn't be sure. They sat side by side, watching the clock on the bookcase that had a Mickey Mouse for a second hand. Mickey was ticking the seconds away. Forty seconds, sixty seconds. Three minutes. Five minutes. Ten minutes. Twenty . . .

The front door bell rang. They heard voices. Philip crept to the door. "My father," he whispered. "My father's home."

His father's voice, and another man's, answering him. The front door slammed. The voices went rumbling on in the hall. On the stairs. His father called, "Philip."

Philip opened his door. "I'm up here." He was astonished to find he could speak.

His father came running up. He was puffing a bit; half frowning, half smiling, as if he wasn't sure how to behave in this situation. There was a policeman behind him. They came into the room and stood there.

"This is my son," Philip's father said. "And his friend, Darcy Jones."

The policeman said, "These the young lads, then?" Although Philip thought this was a silly remark, since his father had just introduced them, he decided that the policeman sounded quite kind. He had a brown, curly beard with soft, pink lips almost hidden inside it. Philip watched his pink lips move and gleam as he said, "What's this you've been up to?"

Philip's father said. "You were seen on the balcony." He stopped and cleared his throat, rather theatrically.

"Correction!" he said. "Someone walking by on the other side of the canal saw a boy with red hair, caught in the spot light. And our neighbour, the lady next door, thought she recognised Philip when you went there, singing carols."

He was warning them not to lie, Philip thought. He supposed he ought to be grateful.

He did his best to look innocent, widening his eyes and speaking in a clear treble. "It was only me in the attic," he said. "I'd climbed in once before because the cat got shut in and was crying. This time it was just a game. Only the alarm went off and it frightened us."

"Breaking into someone's house isn't a game," Philip's father said.

"No," Philip said, "I know it was naughty. And I'm sorry about the door."

"Only about the door?" Philip's father said. He was watching Philip intently.

The policeman said, still speaking kindly, "The lady is very upset, of course. But she admits you were tempted. You were shown a lot of pretty things, weren't you?"

Darcy said, in such a sullen voice it was almost a growl, "We didn't take nothing." He was hanging his head. He shouldn't do that, Philip thought, it made him look guilty. He lifted his own head up bravely.

Philip's father said, "We have to make sure of that, I'm afraid." He looked at the policeman, and smiled, but without amusement. "Do you want to look round? You have my permission."

"It may not be necessary," the policeman said. He waited. Neither boy moved or spoke. Darcy stared at his feet and Philip stared at the Mickey Mouse clock. Mickey ticked merrily backwards and forwards.

At last the policeman spoke. "All right, if that's how you want it! Let's see you turn out your pockets to start with."

Darcy took his jacket off and gave it to the policeman. Then thrust his hands into the pocket of his jeans. He brought out a handkerchief, a pencil sharpener, and a shiny conker with a string through it.

The policeman said, "Tidy pockets for someone your age," and gave him his jacket back. "Now for the other young gentleman."

Philip's first pocket was messy. No handkerchief, only several balled-up damp lumps of Kleenex, some of them pinky-grey from a stub end of chalk; a broken Biro pen, a conker, three badly chipped marbles and a piece of sucked chewing gum dusty with chalk and with bits of hair and thread moulded into it. He put these things down on the bed and his father said, with more anger than he had shown up to now, "I thought I told you not to chew gum, didn't I?"

Philip sighed. He put his hand into his other pocket and felt the coins they had collected this evening. And something else, too. As his fingers closed round it, he felt as if he were falling through space.

"Come on, young man," the policeman said. "Out with it."

"More gum, I expect," Philip's father said. "Filthy habit."

Philip took his hand out of his pocket. He uncurled his fingers and showed them. Three fifty pence pieces, one ten penny piece, and a small ivory Castle.

Chapter 10

When the policeman and Darcy had gone, Philip and his father and Maggie ate supper in dreadful silence. Once or twice, when Philip dared to look up, Maggie smiled comfortingly, but his father didn't look at him until he had finished his steak. Then he pushed his plate away and said, "*Now*—!"

Philip couldn't meet his eyes. He looked at his big nose instead and saw that it was burning red.

His father said, "Have you stolen before, Philip? Or is it your first excursion into crime?"

Philip thought hard. "I once stole some potatoes."

"*Potatoes?*"

"Last month, when they were cutting down those dead trees and burning them by the canal, I stole four potatoes out of the kitchen and we roasted them in the fire. We burned our fingers a bit, but they tasted lovely."

For some reason, remembering how they had tasted, hard-skinned and ashy, made Philip want to cry.

"Potatoes!" his father repeated in a cold, scornful voice. "You know quite well that was not what I meant. I meant, something valuable."

"Potatoes are valuable," Philip said. "A hundred years ago there was a famine in Ireland, and people died because there were no potatoes."

"Please don't try to be clever," his father said. "I was not inviting you to give me a history lesson. I was asking you to be honest with me. Whose idea was it? To break into that house and steal from that poor old woman?"

"She's not poor," Philip said. "She's enormously *rich*. She's got hundreds and hundreds of precious things locked up in that house. Not to use, just to *look* at! It's Addie that's poor, with all the bills she's got to pay, and the baby coming, and Mr Jones needing the electric fire on all the time, and Bing being in prison. And we didn't steal anything. That chess man was a mistake. I picked it up by *mistake*. I'd have told the policeman soon as he asked, only I forgot that I had it."

"That's enough, Philip, thank you," his father said. "You have answered my question."

He stood up, collected his plate and his glass and his knife and his fork and carried them to the dishwasher. This was something he never did normally. When he had fitted the things in the racks, taking a long time about it, he turned back to Philip. "You will not play with Darcy in future. I imagine that his father will agree with me that your friendship has been bad for you both and must not continue. You will go to that school up the road until I can make a more satisfactory arrangement for you, but you will come home the moment your lessons are over and not hang about round the streets as it seems you've been doing. In fact, since it seems you are not to be trusted, Maggie will come to the school and meet you."

Philip stared with hot eyes. "That's not fair."

"You have not been fair to us, have you? We have given you plenty of freedom. We assumed—foolishly, I see now—that you had been brought up to know right from wrong. I am sure that your grandmother thought so. She will be disappointed."

"Don't tell her," Philip said. "Please don't tell her. Oh, *please* . . ." He started to cry. Through his tears, he saw his father smile.

"I'm afraid I will have to tell her," he said, "I can see that will be part of your punishment. Send him to bed, Maggie, will you?"

He left the room. "I hate him," Philip said. Maggie knelt by his chair. Philip leaned against her and wept. He said, "Maggie, I really do hate him. What's going to happen? Where did the policeman take Darcy? Did he take him to *prison*?"

"Of course not, honey," Maggie said, "Little boys don't go to prison. He just took Darcy home. Addie and Mr Jones have got to know what has happened and the policeman will have to talk to them and write a report on the pair of you."

Philip thought of Mr Jones, ranting on, quoting Shakespeare. And the Bible, too, probably. Almost as bad as *his* father! He said, "I should think Darcy would rather have gone straight to prison. I know *I* would, Maggie!"

Nothing happened for three days. They seemed like three years to Philip. Every time he saw a policeman he wanted to run. He didn't see Darcy until Thursday afternoon, on the way home from school.

Darcy was crossing the canal bridge with Addie. Philip only saw his back, walking away. Addie was holding his hand, as Maggie was holding Philip's. Both of them with their jailers.

Maggie said, "Do you want to go and speak to him, honey? You can if you want to," but Philip shook his head.

"I don't think I'd better," he said. "Mr Jones would be angry."

That evening, a policeman came to see Philip. He was older than the one who had caught them, and not wearing a uniform, just a badge on his jacket. He interviewed Philip in his father's study. Maggie was there, but she sat by the door where Philip couldn't look at her. The policeman made Philip stand up while he talked to him. He said that Philip was old enough to understand what crime was. Breaking and entering someone's house was a crime. If

Philip had been older, he could have been sent to a prison for boys. A detention centre, or a reformatory.

Philip said, "My father is going to send me to boarding school. That sounds as bad as prison to me."

Maggie spoke from behind him. She said, "Nothing has been decided yet. Philip's father is trying to decide what is best for him."

"He wants to send me to boarding school as a punishment," Philip said bitterly.

It was hot in the room and his head was aching. The policeman's voice droned on and Philip's mind drifted. He wondered if boarding school would be as bad as in books, all bullies and beatings, and if he would be able to run away. If he could escape, he would go and find Darcy, and they would both run away, as cabin boys to sea . . .

He heard the policeman ask him if he was sorry.

"I suppose so," Philip said. "I'm sorry about the window. I've written a letter to the lady to say so, and I'm going to pay for it to be mended. My father has given the money already and I'm going to pay him back out of my pocket money."

"Your father seems to have the right ideas," the policeman said.

Philip looked at him. He had a wart on one side of his nose. Philip stared hard at this wart and said, "Have you been to see Darcy? Did he say he was sorry? I mean, if I was him, I wouldn't be. He didn't do anything. It was me who got into the house, and it was my fault the window got broken."

"No, I haven't been to see Darcy. We have decided to deal with him in another way." When he had said this, the policeman was silent a moment. Then he said, "This may be hard for you to understand, Philip. Your friend Darcy is appearing in the juvenile court tomorrow morning. Not because he has behaved any worse than you, but because he is older and his circumstances are different. Your father is able to look after you and see that you don't get into trouble again. But the way things are going in Darcy's family, he may need a bit of help from outside if he is to keep on the straight and narrow."

"It's not fair," Philip said.

"Life isn't fair, sonny."

Philip sighed. "That's not what I meant. What I mean is, if Darcy is going to court, then I want to go with him."

It would be a chance to be brave, he thought. He would stand up in the dock as Bing had done, brave and proud, and say, "*I plead guilty.*"

"Then want must be your master, I'm afraid," the policeman said, and smiled as if he had said something funny.

Philip went to school as usual the next day but slipped off mid-morning, hiding in the lavatories until the school bell had rung for the next lesson, then escaping round the back of the buildings and through the hole in the railings.

It was drizzling and cold; his breath steamed through the rain as he ran to the court, and by the time Addie came out of the door, just after twelve o'clock, he was sodden and shivering.

She was alone. Philip ran to her and clutched her. "What's happened? *Where's Darcy?*"

Addie looked down at him. She touched the side of his

face with her finger but she didn't smile. She said, "Nothing bad, Philip. He just has to see the probation officer. He's been put on probation. I'm going to have a coffee while I'm waiting for him. You'd better come with me. You're soaking."

They crossed the road to a café. Addie ordered a cup of coffee with cream for herself, and a milk shake for Philip.

"May I have a mint ice instead?" he asked. Then added, quickly, "As long as it doesn't cost more than the milk, of course."

Addie smiled at him then; her warm smile. "I can afford to buy you a mint ice, my chicken."

The coffee came with a big lump of cream floating on top like a snowy island, and the mint ice had flecks of chocolate in it and a flaky chocolate stick poking out of the top. Philip started on the stick. Addie opened her handbag and took out a packet of cigarettes. She lit one and pulled a face.

"I've never seen you smoke before," Philip said.

"There's a first time for everything."

"But it's bad for your *lungs*. They'll fill up with green pus and you'll *die*."

"I'm not making a habit of it," Addie said. "It was just to help me get through the morning."

Philip said wistfully, "I wish I could have gone to court, too. With Darcy."

"You didn't miss much," Addie said. "It wasn't very exciting."

"It wasn't fair that I couldn't, though. Darcy isn't much older than me."

"I don't think his age was the point," Addie said. "You have a father who is able to take care of you properly. That's how they look at it."

"That's what the policeman said when I asked him. But Darcy's got you, and he's got *his* father."

"A cripple," Addie said. "And a pregnant black woman. And a brother in prison."

"Oh," Philip said. He felt ashamed. "I'm sorry, Addie. I was being silly about wanting to go to the court. I mean, that was childish. But it isn't fair, is it? I mean, the *law* isn't fair. Taking Darcy to court and not me. And sending Bing to prison wasn't fair either, when he had all of you to look after. That was a worse thing than stealing, really. I mean, it was stealing a *person*."

"Don't get into that muddled way of thinking, Philip," Addie said. She stubbed out her cigarette and looked, for a second, both sad and angry. Then she smiled at him. "Let's look on the bright side. Darcy had a fine report from the school. The Headmaster wrote that he was a boy of great promise and character. That was read out in the court for everyone to hear and it did my heart good. And Darcy's pride! He stood up, very tall, and said he was sorry for what he had done, and the magistrate was as kind as he could be. He said he was sure that Darcy had learned his lesson and now he must try and put it behind him. Though I'm afraid his father won't let him forget it so quickly."

"Is he very angry?" Philip asked timidly. "Is he angry with *me*?"

"He is angry with both of you. Darcy has let him down. And he says you should have known better, a boy with your background. But you know Mr Jones. This has been a cruel blow for him, both his sons in this kind of trouble. A blow to his spirit."

"I'm sorry," Philip said.

"He'll rise above it, with God's help," Addie said. "We have to try to look forward and count our blessings, that's what I tell him. Bing out of prison soon, and the baby."

It seemed to Philip that Darcy had more to look forward to than he had. He said, "I've got to go to a boarding school. My father keeps on about it. I don't want to, Addie."

Tears stung his eyes. Addie said, "Don't cry, I don't think I could bear it. Eat your ice-cream instead. It's melting already."

As Philip picked up his spoon, the café door was flung open. His father said, "Philip!" He was wet with the rain and panting as if he'd been running. "They rang from the school and said that you'd disappeared. I was afraid that you'd gone to the court to find Darcy. Then I saw you here, through the window! Eating ice-cream!"

He glared at Philip accusingly; then at Addie. He said, in a cold, formal voice, "I'm sorry, Mrs Jones, but Philip knows perfectly well that he is forbidden to eat sweets between meals."

Philip gasped. This was so rude! A rude, mean thing to say, when Addie had just bought the ice for him!

He looked at Addie for help and saw she was watching his father with a shocked and astonished expression as if she could hardly believe what she had just heard him say. She should tell his father he was being rude, Philip thought. Addie was always so strict about manners! She ought to get *angry*! But she didn't speak to his father. She turned to Philip and said, "Do as he tells you, my chicken. Leave your ice-cream and go with him."

All the way home, running to keep up with his father, Philip wished he could die. There was a pain in his chest, so cold and heavy and hard, he felt that nothing would ever lift it. For the rest of his life it would be there, weighing him down like a stone, growing larger and colder . . .

But when they went into the house, his grandmother was in the hall, holding her arms out. She was wearing her black felt church hat, and her old beaver lamb coat. Too frightened to look at her, Philip sank his face in the ancient fur and smelled camphor.

He could feel her chest and her bones. She was stroking the back of his neck. They went into his father's study and she sat down, still holding him close. She said, "It's all right, Philip. *All right*. Do you hear me?"

He nodded, pressing his face deeper into the coat. He heard his father's voice, muffled by the fur, "Don't make light of it, mother!" and felt his grandmother's ribs move as she sighed. She pushed him away from her, but kept hold of his hand while she spoke to his father.

"I'm not making light of anything, Henry. He has been punished enough, I should think. I have been talking to Maggie. What's this about boarding school? A nine-year-old child? Oh, I can see it might suit you. You're bored with him, so you want to be rid of him, pay someone else for the trouble!"

Philip squeezed her thin fingers, trying to warn her.

He pushed her hat crooked as he whispered into her ear, "*Grandmother*! Don't make him angry!" He stole a quick look at his father and saw, to his surprise, that he was frowning and blushing as if he felt guilty.

His grandmother's pale old eyes snapped. "So you've frightened him, have you? You always were a bully, Henry! Well, you won't bully Philip, not while I have breath in my body, and that will be for a good many years yet."

Philip's father said nothing. His grandmother let Philip's hand go, and put her hat straight. She said, "We are going home, Philip, on the four o'clock train. I have arranged to pay a visit to Mr Jones first, so go and get your things ready now. I have a few things to say to your father."

Maggie was helping him pack. Philip said, "I thought she'd be angry with me. But she was angry with *him*."

"Poor Henry," Maggie said. "He's always been scared of her."

Philip thought that this couldn't really be true. But he didn't say so because Maggie was looking so sad. She said, "You know, honey, your father didn't mean to be unkind. Only he's not used to boys. And he thought that a boarding school might be good for you." She sighed as she folded his shirts. "I shall miss you, Phil, honey."

"I'll miss you," Philip said. And then, because she still looked unhappy, "I expect I'll even miss *him*, just a little."

He would miss them all, he thought; Darcy, and Addie, and Mr Jones, too. He would even miss London. Walking along the canal after lunch, showing his grandmother the lock and the ducks and the best places for fishing, he felt as if he were saying goodbye to a happy part of his life. He told her what Darcy had told him about the narrow boats and how, in the old days before they had engines, the boatmen used to lie on their backs and walk the boats through the tunnels. He thought of a good joke. "You'd have been a good boatman," he said, "with your tunnel vision."

His grandmother laughed. But she knew how he was feeling. She said, "You can come back to visit. The canal won't go away, and I don't suppose Darcy will, either."

"It won't be the same."

"Nothing ever is," his grandmother said. "Things change all the time. You have to get used to it. What are you sighing for, Philip?"

"I was just thinking."

"Thinking what?"

"I don't suppose Mr Jones will let Darcy be friends with me now. Not after what happened."

"Leave Mr Jones to me," his grandmother said. "I think I know how to deal with him."

"He's a very stern man. He says I should have known better."

He looked shyly at his grandmother. Although she had stood up for him in front of his father, she would surely be cross with him now. But she only said, calmly, "Well, you should have done, shouldn't you?"

They rang Addie's bell. She opened the door at once, as if she had been waiting behind it, and Philip's grandmother held out her hands to her. She said, "Oh, my dear, what trouble you've had, I'm so sorry," and Addie made a small sighing sound, a soft, wordless greeting, and put her arms round her.

Mr Jones was in his chair by the fire in the little front room, Darcy standing beside him. Philip's grandmother kissed Darcy and shook Mr Jones by the hand. She said, "Thank you for letting us come, Mr Jones. I'm so glad to be able to meet you."

"It is an honour for us," Mr Jones said. "You must excuse me, not getting up, Mrs Holbein. My legs are in trouble today. But Addie has prepared a small celebration. She has made a sponge cake since you telephoned, and we have a bottle of sherry. Will you take a glass with me?"

"I shall be delighted, Mr Jones," Philip's grandmother said.

She sat beside him. For a little while, they talked about Mr Jones's arthritis and the effect that the weather had on it. Philip's grandmother praised Addie's sponge cake. Philip said, "Addie makes lovely cakes," and Mr Jones looked at him for the first time. His green eyes were sharp and considering.

Philip held his breath, waiting. Then Mr Jones said, speaking to the room at large, "I know one young man who has always enjoyed them."

Philip's grandmother said, "You and Addie have been so good to Philip, Mr Jones. I do thank you. And for letting Darcy come and stay with us last summer. It was such a pleasure for me to see two boys so happy together. Darcy is a fine boy, Mr Jones. But of course you know that. You must be so proud of him!"

Philip saw Addie smile and turn away quickly to hide it. Mr Jones was looking at Philip's grandmother as if he wasn't sure how to answer her.

She said, "I know they have been naughty boys, Mr Jones, but that is all over now, isn't it? My late husband, General Holbein, was always of the opinion that once a man had been punished, that should be the end of it. I hope you will allow Darcy to visit us again at the castle. One should never lose touch with good friends."

Mr Jones seemed to be struggling with himself. His cheek bones grew pink. At last he said, rather reluctantly, "Those friends thou hast, and their adoption tried, grapple them to thy soul with hoops of steel."

Darcy and Philip looked at each other and grinned.

"Shakespeare always puts things so well, I think," Philip's grandmother said. "I'm glad you agree with me, Mr Jones. But to tell you the truth, it is not just for Philip's sake that I want Darcy to come and see us again as soon as he can. I am anxious that he should sing to my friend, Lady Anstruther. She used to be a singer herself, and she would like to hear him. He has a beautiful voice as you know, Mr Jones."

"He gets that from me, Mrs Holbein. When I was a boy, in Wales, I won all the prizes. Like a lark singing, our choir master said. Perfect pitch. And all without training."

"That brings me to my point," Philip's grandmother said. "I hope you won't think me impertinent, but I am an old woman and I'm sure you'll forgive me. Darcy's voice should be trained, Mr Jones. There are schools for boys with good voices and scholarships for them. The cathedral choir schools, and theatrical schools. Lady Anstruther might be able to suggest what would be best for him. She was well known in her day, and she still has connections."

"It would be a fine thing for Darcy if Her Ladyship would be gracious enough to take such an interest," Mr Jones said. His cheekbones were fiery now; small, glowing, red suns. "It would be an honour. What do you say, Darcy?"

Darcy looked at his father, then at Philip's grandmother. He said, "Thank you very much, Mrs H. But it's not for me, really. I mean, I like singing, it's what I like doing best, but if I went to be trained, it would be a long time before I earned anything, wouldn't it? That's got to be thought of. There's Addie and Dad and the baby. It wouldn't be fair to put it all on to Bing. I ought to go in with him, into the business. Bing could do with a partner, when he gets his shop going. Even before I leave school, I can help him. Evenings and weekends, and that. He'll need someone, specially now, after what's happened. I don't know as much about antiques as he does, but I'm better than he is at figures."

He had gone very pale. He looked older, too, Philip thought; almost as if he had grown older while he was speaking. When Philip's grandmother answered him, she sounded tired, as if she had spent all her energy.

"You must make up your own mind, Darcy, naturally. Of course you must think of your family. But you must discuss it with them, with your father and Addie, and with Bing when he comes home."

"I *can't*, Mrs H," Darcy said, almost desperately. "I mean, it's nice *thinking* . . ."

"That's all I'm asking you to do, dear," Philip's grand-mother said. "There's no hurry. Take your time over it. But Philip and I have to go in a minute. Before we do, will you sing for me? One of the songs that I taught you?"

Addie played the piano and Darcy sang *Greensleeves*, and while he sang, Philip looked at them all, at Mr Jones in his chair, Addie on the piano stool with her baby inside her, and Darcy singing to please his grandmother, and felt his heart swell with a strange, disturbing sensation; a happy grief, a sweet, aching longing. He was happy because all the people he loved were here now, in the room with him, and sad because they could not be together for ever.

"I wish," he said, when they had said goodbye and were walking back to his father's house to collect his luggage and go to the station, "I wish . . ." His throat closed up, choking him.

His grandmother said nothing then. But when they were in the taxi, driving round Trafalgar Square, she took his hand and said suddenly, "If wishes were horses, Philip dear, beggars would ride," and this made him laugh. Laughing eased the tight pain in his throat and his chest, and by the time they had got in the train, it was almost quite gone. He looked at his grandmother, settled comfortably in a window seat with her Posture Cushion behind her, and was glad to be going home with her, safe home to their castle.